29 a...

‖‖‖‖‖‖‖‖‖‖‖‖‖‖‖‖‖‖‖‖‖‖‖
⟨⟩ **W9-CQQ-387**

TROUBLE IN TIMBERLINE

Author Of Millions Of Books In Print!

"Brand is a topnotcher!" —*New York Times*

A writer of legendary genius, Max Brand has brought to his Westerns the raw frontier action and historical authenticity that have earned him the title of world's most celebrated Western writer.

In *Trouble In Timberline*, foreman Dan Peary finds the perfect job for ranch hand Barney Dwyer. Peary offers the powerful cowboy a prize mustang and a handful of dollars to bring back his no-account son. Trouble is, Peary's boy has joined up with a gang of ruthless desperadoes who will gun down anyone who comes after him. But no man alive can stop Barney Dwyer when he sets his brains—and his considerable brawn—to a job.

MAX BRAND

TROUBLE IN TIMBERLINE

LEISURE BOOKS **NEW YORK CITY**

A LEISURE BOOK®

October 1995

Published by special arrangement with Golden West
Literary Agency.

Dorchester Publishing Co., Inc.
276 Fifth Avenue
New York, NY 10001

TROUBLE IN TIMBERLINE

Part
One

1

The first drops of rain struck the ground so hard that they knocked up little puffs of alkali dust and filled the air with a clean, pungent scent; but none of the cowpunchers outside the bunkhouse moved. They did not wish to be driven into the airless, stale heat of the room, so they remained sprawling, head and shoulders against the wall and bodies stretched out limply, while they stared gloomily toward the west. That half of the sky was all fire and smoke around a thunderhead larger than a mountain range and constantly rising. Sometimes lightning worked a vein of gold across the foundations of the cloud; and sometimes a gusty wind blew out of the sky and set wheels of dust spinning across the ranch. Everything pointed to rain, but the men continued to smoke their cigarettes in a gloomy silence, waiting for the boss to give commands for the covering of the load of hay, which stood in front of the barn. Getting in winter feed is harder work than riding range, and they were all very tired.

Daniel Peary, who owned that stretch of sand and grama grass from the foothills to the river, had been studying the progress of that cloud even more intently than the rest, yet he

delayed the order to pull a pair of big tarpaulins over the load
of hay. He was a working boss, and his hands were sore from
the haft of a pitchfork; there was a quirk of pain in the
muscles of his back. He understood the temper of his men,
for his mind was as theirs, and he merely said, bantering,
"The rest of us are all tuckered out, Barney, and you're as
fresh as a daisy. Why don't you go and pitch that load of hay
into the barn before the rain gets it wet?"

A reclining cowpuncher gets up very much like a horse,
with a roll to the side and then a heave from hands and knees,
but Barney Dwyer rose without effort, as an Indian will rise,
or a gymnast in the circus. He turned his good-humored face
toward the coming storm and nodded in understanding.

"All right," he said. "I'll throw it off."

He walked to the wagon, caught hold of the lofty edge of
the hayrack, and drew himself up as though the body depending from his hands was not two hundred pounds of bone and
solid muscle but a stuffing of dry straw.

He heard a mutter of laughter behind him. In a sudden flaw
of the wind he distinctly made out the voice of the boss
saying: "He ain't a man, he's a horse!" Barney winced a
little. He was accustomed to contempt, but he never grew
used to it.

He rubbed his big hands together and picked out the
pitchfork, which was stuck in the top of the load like an
ornament on a great pale head of hair. The wild mare had
come to the edge of the corral. Sometimes she looked toward
the storm cloud; sometimes she looked at Barney Dwyer,
with her mane and the silk of her tail rippling out to the wide
in the wind. She seemed to be drawing a deduction from the
cloud and the man with the cunning of her savage brain. And
he stared back at her for an instant with admiration such as he
always felt for creatures who are adequately proportioned in
brain and body. As for himself, he was all body and no brain.
Many a time he had been told so, with curses.

He walked to the edge of the load, grasped the pitchfork,
and leaned back, pulling a great roll of hay, a huge and
increasing poundage, toward the door of the barn. As the

weight increased, as the struggle became greater, a fervor came up in him and burned away.

He was putting almost all of his strength into the labor, but carefully, for he knew that when he was at full strain odd things happened to the tools he used. Axe handles, shovels, new leather reins burst apart. On this very ranch, in the short month of his employment there, he had broken two axes, and a big-bladed crosscut saw, meant for two men to sway, had snapped while he was using it alone. The temper had failed Daniel Peary on that occasion.

"You big flat-faced fool!" he had shouted. "You break anything more on this place, and you're fired. That crosscut saw is worth more than you are. You're a dummy, is what you are!"

Barney Dwyer sighed as he remembered. People were always talking to him like that. And now he used all the care he could in tugging that monstrous roll of hay to the door of the barn and pushing it through.

A drop of rain stung his forehead. It made him hurry his work. Again and again he drove great weights of hay through the barn window.

"Good boy, Barney!" called the cowpunchers, lolling in the dust in front of the bunkhouse. They were all clever experts with rope and gun. When they saw a cow cutting up in the distance, they could tell by its actions what sort of flies were bothering it. They could doctor a sick horse, mend harness, build fence, weave horsehair into ropes and bridles. To see them work, to see what they accomplished with their puny hands, was always a wonder and a delight to him. Therefore, although they laughed as they praised him now, he forgave the laughter and reddened with joy because of the praise.

There was more than a ton of hay on that wagon; he cleared it off with the expedition of a Jackson fork until hardly a quarter of it was left. A volley of rain struck him and put twenty small, cold fingertips upon his skin. He ran to complete his work, dipped the pitchfork deep, and heaved back. Alas, the handle of the fork shattered and broke off close to the tines!

Fear came over him. He saw the boss leap up and run toward the wagon. He dared not face Daniel Peary.

"Get off of that!" shouted Peary. "Get off of that wagon. Get off the ranch. I'm through with you. I never saw such a fool. Get off that wagon."

He climbed down to the ground. After the weight of exertion that he had laid upon himself, his body felt light. He was covered with sweat, and the wind blew him cold all over. But his heart was colder still. Night was coming on, but there was no shadow in night to compare with the darkness of his spirit. He looked down at the ground. All that he saw of Daniel Peary was the hand that he brandished under his nose.

"You're as worthless as that fool of a mustang mare. She's big, too. She's strong, too. And what's she worth? She ain't worth a damn! I'm through with you. I'm gonna pay you off. I owe you forty dollars and I'm gonna give it to you now. You take it and get out. I oughta take off the price of the things you've broke. You've eaten for three and you've broken for ten!"

That freckled fellow, Billy Murphy, sang out: "Give him the mare for part pay. Give him the mare for thirty dollars."

"I'll do it!" shouted Daniel Peary, his rage increasing as his injustice began. "I'll throw in the mare for thirty dollars. Take her. Take her and the old saddle and bridle in the barn. Take the bunch for thirty-five dollars. Take that, or you don't take nothing!"

Barney Dwyer looked sadly toward Murphy. Billy Murphy was clever at everything. He could sew like a woman, sing like a minstrel, do magic tricks with cards. And clever men were always the hardest on Barney Dwyer.

"What would I do with the mare, Mr. Peary?" he asked.

"What would anybody do with a horse? Ride her, you half-wit!" shouted Daniel Peary.

Barney Dwyer shrank again. He could not argue, but he knew that the best horse wranglers in the outfit had been thrown by the wild horse. He knew that they had brought over the Mexican, Juan Martinez, to try his Spanish bit and cruel spurs on her, and she had thrown Martinez twice, and tried to eat him after the second time.

"All right," said Barney. "That only leaves five dollars cash."

The cruelty of Daniel Peary waxed as he saw his victim submissive.

"You'll get that five dollars by walking for it," he said. "Walk up to that town of Timberline and find my son Leonard. Len owes me more'n five dollars. He can pay you five. Wait a minute. I'll give you an order on him."

He snatched out a little notebook with a sweat-stained red cover. With a pencil he scribbled a note.

"Take that!" he said, thrusting into Barney's hands the page on which he had written.

Barney Dwyer went into the bunkhouse and rolled his pack. There was not enough of it to take long. He rolled the pack long and lean and hard and then walked out into the red of the sunset and the silence of the men. He was surprised to find that they were not laughing at him. Strange to say, they were all frowning at the ground, biting their lips. And Daniel Peary walked up and down in as black a rage as ever, never glancing at his hired hands.

Barney went along the line and shook hands. He was amazed again. They all stood up. They all gripped his hand heartily.

Billy Murphy said: "I'm sorry, kid! I've got a couple of bucks. Here, you take that along with you!"

He held it out. Others were reaching for money, too, and Barney Dwyer backed away from them, overwhelmed with embarrassment, crushed by their kindness.

"I wouldn't be needing that," said Barney Dwyer. Tears came into his eyes. He choked. He felt that in all the world there were no men so noble, so good, so kind as these. "I'll be getting five dollars up there in Timberline," said he. "But I'll remember that you've offered it to me. I'll never forget that. I'll remember you all, because I see that you're my friends!"

As the fullness of this delightful conviction came over him, it forced back his head a little, and the sunset flushed on his face as he smiled at them.

He offered his hand to Daniel Peary, saying: "I'm sorry

that I've broken things. I guess I've broken about as much as my pay would come to. Maybe I'd better not take the mare?"

"Take the mare and be damned," said Peary, and turned his back.

To that lean back, somewhat bowed by riding and many labors, Barney said, with a sigh: "I wanted not to break things, and I'm sorry. If I had a chance to do anything to make up, I'd like to do it."

Suddenly Peary whirled around on him.

"There's one thing you can do for me, and if you break his neck handling him, I don't care! Take my son Len and drag him out of Timberline from that gang of crooks and put him back here on the ranch, where he belongs. Go on and do that for me—and I'll give you another horse as good as that!"

He snapped his fingers at Barney Dwyer and strode off toward the ranch house, while Barney went into the barn and took the bridle, the old, battered rag of a saddle with the rope coiled on its horn, and went out into the corral.

He had to corner the mare half a dozen times before he managed to rope her, for she dodged like a cat and made a game of it. However, she knew a rope if she knew nothing else, and once the noose was around her neck she stood quietly and let him put on the saddle and bridle. The cowpunchers stood along the corral fence, laughing, giving advice. He had no hope of being able to ride her when so many better men had failed, but nevertheless it was his duty to try. So he climbed into the saddle.

Sitting in that saddle was like sitting down on the end of a flying piston rod. With the power of his knees he crushed the big mustang till she grunted. Then he rose high in the air and came floundering down on hands and knees.

When he got up, the mare was standing in a corner of the corral, playing with her bit, cocking her ears at him.

"Next time you go up, bring us down a nice cool chunk of that cloud, Barney, will you?" called someone.

They began to shout and laugh. They kept up that shouting and laughing while the red bay mare shed him six more times from her back, and finally slammed the length of his body against the wall of the barn.

He lay in the dust, stunned, till Billy Murphy and another

man ran to pick him up. They thought he might have broken his back or fractured his skull, but he stood up and shrugged his shoulders as he started for the mare again.

"What's the use, Barney?" said Murphy. "She'll kill you if you keep it up. What's the use?"

"Don't you think I'd better keep on trying?" asked Barney.

"Not unless you're made of India rubber."

"I guess I'll stop trying, then," sighed Barney Dwyer, "because I'm not made of rubber."

They laughed loudest of all at that, but he forgave them easily. They had offered him their money, all of them; and he would never forget.

He led the mare out of the corral.

"Hey!" said Billy Murphy. "You come back in here and sleep, tonight. Not even a dog oughta be run off on a night like this, with a storm coming on!"

"I wouldn't stay," said Barney. "The boss wouldn't like it. He wouldn't like to have me stay around on the place."

So he shook hands once more with Murphy and headed straight into the foothills, toward the mountains. It would take him two days to get to Timberline, probably. His chances of eating along the way were very slender. And he had with him, for capital, exactly five dollars in a note that had to be collected.

The night came down on him as he climbed the hills, and the long-promised rain was on him with a rush and a roar, filling the darkness with sound as a river fills a narrow stone canyon. He thought of turning the mare loose, since she was useless to him. But as the thunder boomed over them and the lightning sprang, she pressed up to his shoulder for comfort. He stroked her face and went on, glad of that companionship.

2

The world of dust and grama grass turned into a world of mud. He could not pause to rest unless he lay down in the wet, so he slopped on, stepping blindly most of the time. He would have lost the trail before long. It was the mare who kept to it, steadily, so he let her have her way.

Presently she began to act as though she were alone, not under the guidance and the chaperonage of the man. If a strange scent reached to her downwind, she paused, and Barney stopped beside her, admiring her manner of lifting her head and studying danger that was to him unguessed. Once or twice she stopped to sniff at the ground. Once she shied suddenly far to the left and almost tore the lead rope from his hand. This wilderness of night was to her a book which she could read clearly and well, while to him it was a black wall that he leaned his head against, to no purpose.

But Barney had given over wondering why God had given to him nothing but the strength of his hands, and to all other creatures some special blessing of mind and spirit. He looked up to this wild, brave horse. She was all iron and fire. What was this night of storm to her, when she had known how to brave four or five lonely winters on the range, pawing away the snow to get at the grass?

The thought of this gave Barney a sudden warmth of confidence. For if she could take such good care of herself, she was not apt to lead him into trouble. It was better, therefore, to let her go ahead on a loose rope.

They came to steeper hills and slopes where he could be glad that fatigue was such a stranger to him. Then they reached the lowest belt of the lodgepole pines and from these passed into great forests on a trail that had grown into what could almost be called a road.

That road dipped out of the forest into a ravine that was filled with a sound of rushing like a great wind, but there was no stir of air through most of its length. It was merely the pouring of water that swept down the valley. The trail was looped along the rocky wall of the ravine. Sometimes it was safe enough. Sometimes horse and man had to go in single file. At those moments, Barney let the mare go first on a length of the rope, for her footing of the dangerous places held up a light for him to follow.

Over his head, the lightning ripped from sky to earth,

sometimes lighting the whole range and showing him the three mountains that, he knew, rose near the town of Timberline. By that he could be sure that they were on the right trail, though he never had traveled it before.

Those same lightning flashes always showed him the mare, as she went busily up the trail, never hesitant, except when some narrowing of the trail threatened to leave no footing at all between the wall of the gorge and the water beneath.

They came to the waterfall. Driftings of the spray blew into his face. All the rocks of the ravine wall and the trail were gilded with water. It was a place to watch every step. Yet the mare went steadily up the steepness of the way until they had gained the top. There was no longer a ravine, merely a valley with wooded hills rolling back on either side. Exactly then, luck failed them.

They had just passed the lip of the falls when the bank crumbled under the feet of the bay mare and she dropped into a current that was whipping toward the precipice like a flight of arrows. One instant she was before Barney; the next, she was gone, and the rope burned through his hands to the final knot.

On that he glued the strength of his grip and was jerked into the margin of the stream. But on an elbow of rock he hooked his left arm, and endured the strain. By the lightning he saw the mare struggling at the end of the rope, her head lost to him in the flinging water, most of the time. But when he glimpsed it, he saw that the ears were still pricked! Just beyond her, the river bent down to make its long plunge.

Little by little she worked in toward the bank. It might be that she could reach it and clamber up. It might be that the bank was sheer. In that case, it was merely a question of how soon his endurance might give way. In the meantime, the snow-water froze him to numbness.

He dropped his chin on his chest and grinned with agony. Between his shoulder blades, the muscles seemed to be giving way, but still his grip remained on the knot.

He told himself that he would count to ten, and then let go. He counted to ten, and hung on. He counted to ten again. He counted many times, but still he could not surrender that

grasp, which was the life of the mare. That was what he was
doing, he told himself. He was holding a life in his hand. She
was brave, she was beautiful, she was strong, and all of her
lay in the grip of his hand! It was like being God for one
creature; but ah, the agony of that being!

Then the rope jerked violently. The strain ceased. He
thought that the strands must have parted, but looking up, he
saw the red mare on the ledge above him.

Slowly he clambered out. He sat for a time on the very
edge of the bank, where it had crumbled, until by degrees the
warmth of his strength returned to him. He rose. The mare
trembled with cold and exhaustion. Her head was hanging.
Therefore Barney found a sheltered place among the pine
trees. With twists of the pine needles he rubbed her dry,
tethered her to a sapling, then wrung out his own clothes,
which were soaking, pulled them on again, and into heaped
up leaves and pine needles he crawled and slept.

The sense of the storm remained with him all night, but in
the morning he found a brilliant sky with only enough white
clouds steering through it to set off the blue. The world
burned with life. Every rock glistened. The trees were a
shimmering green. When Barney Dwyer walked up the valley, from meadow to meadow and from grove to grove, it
seemed to him that there was nothing ugly or dangerous on
earth except the men who inhabit it.

The mare was quite herself again. She was gayer than the
birds or the leaping of the water in the river. When they came
to a green plateau of rolling ground, it seemed to Barney that
no crime could be greater than to keep such a wild thing
enslaved. So he stripped off saddle and bridle and rope. He
swung the rope with a shout, and off she went, a red ray of
speed that disappeared around the shoulder of the next hill.

He looked after her, long after she was gone, then settled
saddle and bridle and rope in the fork of a tree before he went
on. He was very hungry, by this time, so he paused to tighten
his belt. He had heard in his boyhood that Indians found this
a comfort in days of famine. It never had been a comfort to
him, but he always followed the practice when he was
starving. When at last he was ready to start up the valley

toward the three mountains of Timberline, he saw the red mare not twenty yards away, cropping the grass.

Bewilderment made him take off his hat to the sun and the wind. She had returned! But perhaps it was merely as the wild hawk will dip down from the upper air in scorn of the hunter. He walked straight up to her, holding out his hand, and she, pretending not to see him, kept her head turned until the last instant. Then she was gone like quicksilver from the touch. She fled in a circle, brandishing her heels in the air. At last she paused, near him, and with legs well planted, ready to dodge him in any direction, dared him to come on. But still Barney laughed. Without hesitation, with a strength of conviction, he walked straight up to her and put his hand on her shoulder; but she merely lifted her head and turned fearless eyes on him, as one who might say, "Well, what of it?"

He took her by the mane, and led that red thunderbolt back to the tree, where he saddled and bridled her, put the rope on her neck, and then tied it to the horn of the saddle. After that, he walked straight into the valley with excitement bubbling like a fountain of wine in his heart.

He began to talk to her as he never had talked to a human being. In a short time, his whistle stopped her wherever she was running. When he spoke and held out his hand, she would come curiously up to him.

So he forgot the miles. He forgot his hunger. He could not stop smiling all the way through the uplands, while the three great mountains drew closer above him, their blue-white heads shining in the sky.

He reached timberline, and looking down into a great hollow where the trees began again and a stream angled through their midst, he saw a small village. On three sides of it the three mountains looked down, so he knew that he was at the town of Timberline at last. He took out the folded bit of paper torn from the notebook. Water had blurred the writing, but it was still decipherable. With that paper fluttering in his fingers, and with the red mare crowding up to his heels, he came out of the happy wilderness.

3

It was a very small town, but complete after the Western fashion, with a general merchandise store, hotel, blacksmith shop, and three saloons.

Half a dozen boys playing in a vacant lot pointed their fingers at the stranger and the red mare and shouted and laughed. No matter how accustomed he was to shouts and laughter, the iron entered freshly into the soul of Barney Dwyer; he had been free from pain so long that he had forgotten some of its quality.

On the veranda of the hotel sat one tall, stark man with his hands laid out on his knees, his eyes fixed far off on the darkness of his thoughts.

"Can you tell me where I can find Leonard Peary?" asked Barney.

The other drew his glance away from the distance and examined Barney Dwyer without interest. Then he returned to his reflections.

"I said," repeated Barney more loudly, "can you tell me where I can find Leonard Peary?"

A faint smile appeared on the lips of the man on the veranda. That was the only answer.

Barney turned helplessly away. Down the street a yellow sign hung over a pair of saloon doors, and to that place he went. He tied the mare to the hitching rack and went inside. Half a dozen men were at the bar, talking quietly. Barney stepped up to the deserted end of the counter and faced his image in the mirror. His throat and face looked a little sleek, but not exactly boyish. Between his eyes there was a line of trouble.

The bartender made a step toward him.

"Yours, stranger?" he asked.

"I can't buy a drink, I—" began Barney.

"No handouts here for bums," said the bartender.

14

"I only wanted to ask a question," said Barney.

"Shoot, then."

"I wanted to know if you can tell me where to find a man called Leonard Peary in this town?"

The bartender elevated his brows, turned his head, and looked toward one of his customers. He was a darkly handsome fellow, young, with a pair of restless bright eyes that see everything at a glance. He nodded now toward Barney Dwyer.

"You want me?" he asked.

"I've got a note, here, from your father," said Barney.

He came up and held out the scrap of paper. Leonard Peary read it, reflected for an instant, and then drew out a wallet. He continued to talk to the others. And they hung upon his words, already smiling before they heard the point of the tale. They seemed to Barney a formidable lot of manhood, and yet it was plain that they were mere attendants upon this paladin. Everything set him apart. The very clothes he wore had a half Mexican dash and color about them. His peaked sombrero made him seem as foreign as his swarthy complexion; the flash of his smile was wholly Latin, too.

So, still talking, he drew out a bill, stiffened it with a little jerk, and so extended it toward Barney without turning his head.

"Thanks!" said Barney. "Thanks a lot! Sorry to bother you, but—"

Leonard Peary talked on, carelessly. Not one of his audience had so much as a glance to waste on the stranger. So Barney Dwyer went hastily out of the saloon. The mare danced and neighed impatiently as she saw him, but Barney stood, overcome by a memory. Had not Daniel Peary told him to bring back his son to the ranch, even by the nape of the neck?

As well think of bringing a beautiful black panther out of the woods with naked hands! Yet such a command had a weight with Barney. He always had tried to obey orders with a literal exactness. And now it seemed to him that if he brought the son back to the ranch, would there not be a rejoicing and gratitude?

So, on the instant, he fixed in his mind the great determination. He would have to eat, rest, and think over the project first.

He untethered the mare and went down the street with her at his heels. He left her outside the merchandise store, untied, while he went in to buy food. He found a counter running around three sides of the room to accommodate purchasers of hardware or groceries or of clothes. In the center of the open floor rose a big stove, girt with a nickeled rail on which heels could be rested in winter. Half a dozen chairs were at hand, but they had been hitched around to face the central counter. There was the presiding clerk, a girl, whose bare arms were folded as she chatted with the loiterers. She was so pretty that Barney, the instant he stood inside the door, dragged off his hat. He felt that the haste of the gesture had made his blond hair stand on end.

And one of the trio, half turning toward him, jerked a thumb to his shoulder to indicate the stranger. "Hey, look at!" said he. They chuckled, all of them. How strange, thought Barney, that they were able to see, with the first glance, that he was a fit subject for derision.

As he approached the counter, the girl straightened.

"Why are you laughing, Riley?" she demanded briskly. "*You* wouldn't know enough to take off your hat, even if you were in church!"

At this rebuke, they laughed all the more, and loudly.

And big Riley, lolling in the chair, exclaimed: "Is this a church, Sue?"

Barney waited for her to answer that question, but she kept her brown eyes fixed on him, expectantly, and took no more heed of the three, or of Riley's question.

"I'd like to get some flour and bacon," said Barney. "And some fish hooks and a line. And some salt and baking powder. And"—he looked down to the torn left sleeve of his flannel shirt, where it had been ripped—"and a needle and some thread," he concluded. He looked up at her from his sleeve. She was smiling, a twisted smile that made him blush.

"He's gunna set up housekeeping," said Riley. "That's like a married man, giving an order! That's what it is!"

"Oh, no," said Barney, for he felt that the words should be answered. "I'm not married."

They crowed with delight and examined Barney with a bright pleasure, beginning to hope for more sport.

"You be quiet, all the three of you," said the girl. Yet Barney saw that she, too, would have liked to laugh. "How much of all these things do you want?"

Barney tried to think in pounds and numbers, but his mind was struck with confusion. He wanted only to get out into the street again as soon as possible.

"I don't know," he told her, making a vague gesture with both hands. "About three dollars' worth, if you don't mind."

He spread the five-dollar bill on the edge of the counter and waited.

"Well," said the girl, "if you don't know—oh, all right. I'll get everything together. Three dollars, eh?"

"Who's your father, boy?" asked Riley.

"My father is dead," said Barney.

The girl was busy, her brown hands flashing here and there.

"Let him alone, Riley!" She exclaimed, but without turning from her rapid work. "Let him alone! It isn't fair!"

"And a frying pan—not a big one," said Barney.

That seemed to amuse everyone more than all that had passed before. The girl was laughing, too, as Barney could tell from the movement of her shoulders. She struck that laughter from her face before she turned to the counter again, yet her eyes were still shining with it. She put all the desired articles in a heap.

"Is that all?" she asked.

"That's all," said Barney. "How much, please?"

"It's two dollars and eighty-five cents—if that's enough flour."

"That's do fine," said Barney, and presented the bill.

She took it, opened the cash drawer, and then paused. She frowned as she stared at Barney.

"That money is no good. That's counterfeit," said she.

He, in a trance, saw the greenback being pushed across the counter toward him. He accepted it and turned it back and forth without understanding.

"Counterfeit?" said he blankly.

"It's too bad," answered the girl. "I'm sorry. Who gave it to you?"

"Why, a man named Leonard Peary gave it to me," said Barney.

"He wouldn't do such a thing!" cried the girl.

"He's a liar!" exclaimed Riley, jumping up from his chair. "Len Peary never gave you that!"

He advanced on Barney with arm outstretched, pointing. Behind, came his two companions, with happy looks, intent on mischief.

"I don't suppose Peary knew it was bad money," said Barney. "Only—it was he who gave it to me! I'm sorry!"

"You'll be sorrier when we throw you out of town. We're gunna give you a run, brother!" cried Riley.

Barney shrank back from that advance of the three.

"Don't touch me," he exclaimed. "Don't—"

"Let him alone!" exclaimed the girl. "He's not worth it—the great baby!"

"Grab him, boys!" said Riley. "We'll show him the rough side of Timberline."

They closed in on Barney with a sudden, happy shout and a rush. This was what he dreaded more than all else in the world. For if pitchfork handles of stoutest hickory will snap like straws, how can fragile bones of arms and legs be expected to endure a sudden wrench?

With a sweep of his arms he staggered two of them backward. The driving fist of Riley he picked out of the air, caught his other wrist, and crossed his arms across his breast.

"Help!" shouted Riley. "He's breaking my arms! He's—"

"I don't want to hurt you," said Barney, instantly relaxing his grip. "I'm sorry I hurt you. Only, you all came at me. I sort of had to do something. I'm sorry!"

One of them was rubbing the side of his cheek where the back of Barney's hand had landed in the first gesture. And big Riley was looking down at his wrists as though they were in fact broken. But all three of them began to back toward the door. The two went out first. Riley lingered to shout: "But I'm comin' back! I'm comin' back—and clean you up!"

Then he vanished in turn.

Barney Dwyer, following toward the door, still held out a hand, as though in fact he were approaching a horse. He kept saying, "I didn't mean it! I didn't want to hurt you—"

But when the door slammed hastily as he came closer, he turned back toward the girl and made a helpless gesture.

"I'm afraid they went away because of me," said Barney. "I'm sorry!"

"Don't be sorry," said the girl. "Sit down and tell me about yourself, will you?"

4

To Barney, it was as though he had been chosen from multitudes, and by a queen, but he saw that there was no glow of pleasure in her.

"Is it another of Leonard's little tricks?" she asked. "Did he send you here?"

"Leonard Peary?" he asked, amazed. "Why, no."

"He gave you the counterfeit money, you say?" she asked.

"Yes, but—"

"And you just *happened* to come straight here? It wasn't that he wanted to see if my eyes were really open so that I could tell good money from bad?"

"Oh, no," said Barney Dwyer, beginning to suffer in quite a new way.

"It was just by chance, then?" said the girl. "And I suppose it was just by chance that you sleight-handed those three big fellows into helplessness?"

"I have a lot of strength in my hands," he told her, "more than most people have, at least. That's all there was to it. I'm sorry that I hurt them."

She sighed and shook her head, seeming to deny all that he said.

"Will you tell me your name?" she asked.

"Barney Dwyer."

"Alias what?" she asked.

"I don't know what you mean," answered Barney. "You seem to think there's something strange about me. You seem to think that Leonard Peary sent me here. But I don't even know your name."

"It's as plain a name as yours. Susan Jones. But there's a difference. My name is real."

"But so is mine," said Barney. "What do you think I am?"

"I think you're a confidence man," said the girl. "And you've come up here to join Big Mack."

"Confidence man—Big Mack. I don't understand!" said he.

Coldly her eyes examined him.

"You keep your face well," she said. "It's all very cleverly done. But I'm not an admirer. I've seen too much crookedness since I came to Timberline!"

Every word struck him to the heart.

"You think that I'm clever? You think that I'm a crook?" cried Barney Dwyer. "But I'm not! I'm only a ranch hand, and I came up here to collect some money from Leonard Peary. I came from his father's ranch to collect five dollars."

She started; her color grew brilliant for a moment.

"You rode all the way from the Peary ranch?" she exclaimed. "And for five dollars?"

"No. I didn't ride. I walked."

She folded her arms and leaned against the shelves behind the counter.

"Go on," she said. "I'll try to listen. Only—I don't see the point, so far! You say you walked—and yet I can see your horse in the street outside that window!"

"Yes, that's my horse," he agreed. "But I can't ride her. Nobody can. She's wild, d'you see?"

He came a little closer to her, trying desperately, pouring out his spirit to convince her.

"What a fool you must think I am!" said the girl. "And

Leonard must think so, too, or he wouldn't have sent you here!''

"Peary didn't send me here," Barney insisted. "It was Daniel Peary who sent me up here to collect five dollars. He gave me a note, telling Leonard to pay me. So I came up. I brought the mare with me. Please believe what I say!''

Coldly she eyed him. "You walked clear through the mountains to collect five dollars; and the five dollars was paid you in counterfeit. It's quite a story," said the girl.

"But it's all true!" cried Barney. He rose on tiptoe as he realized the vanity of his words. "And Daniel Peary told me to bring his son back from the mountains, if I could. If I did that, would you believe what I've told you?''

"Daniel Peary told you to take Len Peary out of the mountains and back to the ranch? Oh, yes! If you manage that, I'll believe you. Certainly I'll believe you!''

"Then I'll do it, somehow. Even if they kill me while I'm trying.''

"How brave, how simple, how naive!" said the girl, sneering.

"I'd better go," said Barney feebly.

He got to the door and turned there, to look back toward her.

"It's wrong," he managed to say at last. "We ought to be friendly, and not hostile.''

"We're going to see a good deal of one another, are we?" she asked.

"How can I tell that?" asked Barney.

"You know that Leonard Peary sees me nearly every day. If you're one of his companions, I suppose I'll have to be seeing you, too.''

"Does he mean a lot to you?" asked Barney.

In her anger and disdain it seemed that she would not even answer him for a moment.

Then she broke out, "He means so much to me that I wish he were out of these mountains and away from every man like—''

She paused, frowning. "From every man like you!" had

been plainly in her mind, but she left the last accusing word unspoken.

Barney Dwyer sighed.

"You want him away?" he repeated. "You really would like to have him away from Timberline—back on his father's ranch, say?"

"Yes!" she exclaimed. "Back on the ranch raising some honest callouses on his hands. I'd rather see him there than anything in the world. Go tell him that, and let him laugh and sneer with you."

Barney tried to speak again. He wanted to tell her that he would try to accomplish what she wished. But words so failed him that he could only turn from her and stumble blindly out through the door and into the dazzle of the open daylight.

Barney came to the saloon before which the sign swayed slowly back and forth in the wind and there, as he paused, an eager youngster touched his elbow.

"Can I hold your horse, mister?" he asked.

"Thanks," said Barney. "Of course you can hold her!"

"*I'll* take care of her," said the boy, proudly.

"But don't try to ride her," said Barney. "Nobody can ride her. She's full of tricks."

As he passed through the doors of the saloon, he heard the youngster crying out behind him: "Back up, all you gents! *I'm* watchin' after this mare!"

There was a clattering of many voices inside the saloon, but as he appeared, all of that noise ended.

"There he is, now!" said a whisper.

All faces turned toward him with a single white flash. Silently they regarded him. Neither head nor hand stirred. The bartender was transfixed, unable to move with the bottle that he held.

"I'm sorry to bother you," said Barney. "But do you know where Leonard Peary is?"

"It ain't any bother, sir," said the bartender. "I'd right sure tell you where he is, only I don't know. Maybe he'd be out at the Walsh place. He goes there a lot. You know where the Walsh place is?"

The grace of this extreme courtesy amazed Barney.

"I don't know where the Walsh place is," he said. "I'm a stranger here."

The bartender hurried from his place of business toward the door.

"You ain't so strange to Timberline as you was a while ago," he said with a happy unction. "It takes us a while to get to know a man like you, sir. But after a coupla lessons we learn pretty fast!"

He chuckled. Everybody in the room chuckled also, softly.

"A feller like Riley Quintin, maybe he learned all he wanted to know in *one* lesson," said a voice. Subdued laughter welcomed the sally. All faces beamed upon Barney Dwyer. The bartender was ushering him through the swinging doors. He stood in the street, where his white apron flamed in the sun.

"There's the Walsh place, over yonder. Right toward Mount Baldy. It's the only house in sight. You can't miss it!"

Barney Dwyer thanked him and started down the street, with the mare following at his heels.

5

The sun had not set, but it was behind the western peaks and blackened them, particularly the great pyramid of Mount Baldy. The world was all dazzling light or deep shadow. And it seemed to Barney as though he were walking over the crown of the universe, held up where the truth could be seen clearly. Yet the truth about Barney Dwyer had not appeared, as yet, to the people of Timberline! They had seen through him clearly enough, when he entered the place, but now all was changed. They regarded him with respect so profound that he could not think it hypocrisy. Even the girl, for all the clearness of her eyes, seemed to look upon him as a force, as a clever rogue playing a part too deep for her to comprehend entirely.

He was pondering over these things with trouble in his mind, when he heard the scattering of gravel under the hoofs of a trotting horse, and a rider loomed the next moment around the bend of the trail. He was a trim fellow of middle age, with sandy moustache cut short.

He stopped his horse near Barney and waved his hand in a half-military salute. Barney felt authority and halted at once.

"Where you bound, stranger?" asked the man of the moustache.

"Up yonder," said Barney. "The Walsh place."

"Ah," said the other. "You a friend of Bunny Walsh?"

"No, I've never seen him. I've never been in Timberline before. I'm a stranger here."

"I'm the sheriff. My name is Elder," said the other. "What do you want with Bunny Walsh?"

"Oh, are you the sheriff?" said Barney. He looked on Sheriff Elder with awe. People such as sheriffs do not ride into one's life every day. "I'm going up to ask about a man called Leonard Peary."

"Ah," said the sheriff. "You want to see Peary, do you? You want to see Big Mack, too, I suppose?"

It was not the first time that Barney had heard this name. He wondered at it.

"Will you tell me who Big Mack is?"

"You never heard of John McGregor?" asked the sheriff.

"Just a moment," said Barney. He used that moment to look with frowning intentness into his memory. John McGregor seemed a familiar name, yet he could not place it. "No, I don't remember hearing of him."

"Never heard of the devil, perhaps. What's your name?"

"Barney Dwyer. I've heard of the devil, of course," said Barney. "Why do you ask?"

The sheriff grunted.

"I see," he remarked. "You're the sort that plays the simpleminded part, and you do it damned well; though you'll probably be damned doing it!"

"I don't understand," murmured Barney.

"You don't, don't you? But I tell you that you *do* understand. You want Peary, and you're going to the Bunny Walsh place. That's enough proof that you're one of 'em. Enough proof for a hanging, if I could have my way about it. And I'll tell you this, as I've told the rest of 'em! I'm going to wipe the lot of you off the face of the earth one of these days. It's going to be your life or mine. You fellows have murdered some of the people that went before me, and you've bought up the rest. But you won't bury me. And as for the killing, it's a game I know how to play. Goodbye. But remember that I've got my eye on you!"

He rode on down the trail, and Barney Dwyer turned to watch him. He was aggrieved. It was the duty of the law to stand by fellows like himself, he thought, fellows who are not quite as clever and sharp as other men. But now, with a sudden and brutal gesture, he was thrown out in the nakedness of his soul, among the men of Timberline.

Before him lay a sweep of Alpine meadow closely carpeted with low-growing furze and misted over with the color of millions of obscure flowers. On those flowers the bees were at work, all their songs gathered into a voice like far-off violins.

Then he saw the house. It stood up like a gray fist in the midst of the furze, a cloud of big bushes rolling at its feet. When he came up to it, he saw that it was big enough to have served as a hotel, but time and rough weather had battered it, knocked in the windows, stripped patches of shingles off the roof, and peeled and tarnished the paint. Some of the windows were boarded up against storms. In other places, oiled silk would let in some light.

He stepped onto the veranda. Loose boards rattled under his feet. At the door, he rapped and heard the echo sound inside.

While he waited, he turned. The red mare was in the middle of the path, sometimes stealing forward, sometimes shrinking back, as though she were afraid that danger might leap out at her like a snake from any crevice.

After a time, a step came slowly inside the building, the lock clanked, and the door was pulled gradually open, until Barney saw an old, bent black man on the threshold.

"Yes, sir?" he said.

"I want to see Leonard Peary," answered Barney. "Is he here?"

"Mr. Peary ain't here, sir," said the man.

"You can't tell me where to find him?"

"No, sir."

A voice not far away said: "Bring him in, Wash."

Wash stepped back to show the way.

"Mr. McGregor says will you kindly come in, sir?" he invited.

Compared with the rosy brilliance of the outer day, the hall was as dark as the mouth of a trap, and inside it was the chief whom the men of Timberline called Big Mack, the enemy called John McGregor by the sheriff. Barney thought of all this and then promptly went inside.

There was still a gleam of varnish on the bannisters that turned twice in climbing from the shadowy hall, and the masks of some old hunting trophies showed their teeth at Barney. That was all he saw before Wash took him through a pair of double doors into the next room.

At a small table in the center of the room, eating a thick slab of steak from a platter piled with fried potatoes in the margins, sat the austere figure of the man he had seen before on the veranda of the Timberline hotel; that same fellow who had failed to answer his question. It was he who had just spoken to Wash. Therefore he must be Big Mack, that leader of crime in those mountains.

Eyeing Barney, McGregor placed a bit of meat in his mouth and chewed it slowly. Big Mack would have been handsome, thought Barney, except for certain hard angles in his face and the grimness of his expression.

Now he nodded toward a chair.

"Sit down!" said McGregor.

Barney merely rested his hand on the back of the chair that had been indicated. He felt more nervous than ever. Somehow, the loneliness of this meal and the unusual hour of it convinced him that Big Mack was capable of anything.

"Sit down!" ordered McGregor again.

"I'm all right this way," said Barney.

McGregor continued to eat.

"You know who I am?" he asked after a moment, during which time Barney did not dare to speak.

"I think that you're John McGregor," said he.

McGregor lifted dull eyes toward him.

"What makes you think that?"

"After you spoke, a minute ago, Wash said that Mr. McGregor wanted to see me."

"Wash is an old man. He's an old fool," said McGregor without heat. "Wash!"

The servant came through the door, bending forward in haste.

"More whiskey!" said McGregor, instead of speaking the reproof that Barney expected. "And another glass."

"I don't drink whiskey," said Barney.

McGregor, at this, lifted his head and stared calmly, coldly, curiously at Barney. From a stone jug, Wash poured three fingers of amber liquid into a tumbler. McGregor swallowed half of it instantly. He asked for no chaser after it. The sting of that raw liquor brought not a tear into his eyes. His throat was unclouded with huskiness as he said: "You don't drink whiskey?"

"No," repeated Barney.

"Why not?" asked the unemotional voice.

"Well," said Barney, "supposing that I liked it, I wouldn't be able to buy it most of the time. And I get along with water or coffee pretty well."

"You wouldn't be able to buy whiskey, eh?" said Big Mack, continuing to eat. "Why wouldn't you be able to buy whiskey?"

"I'm out of a job a lot of the time," said Barney.

"So am I," said Big Mack, with the smaller half of a smile. "But I can buy whiskey."

"You see," explained Barney, "I don't often have a chance to work more than a month at a time."

"Neither do I," said Big Mack. "What's your game? And who are you?"

"My name is Barney Dwyer. I haven't any game."

"Look here, Dwyer, you do the trick very well. You could

pass as a simpleminded fellow with most people. But I'm not such a fool. Don't take me for a fool. Take me for anything else you please, but don't take me for a fool."

"I won't," said Barney.

"Riley Quintin is a reasonably hardy lad," said Big Mack. "He talks too much and he bawls out everything that's on his mind, but he's a good man with his hands. He had two others with him. You made one move, tied all three of 'em in knots, and threw them out of the store. And yet you come here and try to pretend—"

"I didn't throw them out of the store!" protested Barney. "They walked out. I was sorry to hurt them. They sort of rushed at me, and I had to protect myself. I didn't want to do them any harm!"

McGregor rolled the rest of the whiskey over his tongue, watching Barney constantly over the edge of the glass. Then he pointed, and Barney, looking through an open window at the end of the room, saw the red mare moving uneasily from side to side in front of the house.

"You can afford to buy a horse like that, but you can't afford whiskey, eh?"

"She was given to me," said Barney. "She was—"

"Ah? People will give you horses like that, will they? Because they take a sudden liking to you, eh? They say: 'Dwyer, I never saw you before, but I like you. I want you to remember me. I have a red bay mare in the barn. She cost me a couple of thousand dollars, but I want you to have her. Take her, Barney Dwyer, and use her well, and think of me!' I suppose people talk to you like that, eh?"

"No, no," said Barney. "She's just a wild-caught mare, and she was given as part pay of my wages the other day. She isn't worth much, because nobody can ride her. She's really wild."

"Ah?" said Big Mack. "You keep her along for company, eh?"

"She's pretty good to have along," said Barney, "and—"

"That's going too far! You take me for a half-wit, do you?"

"No, no!" said Barney, in a misery of confusion. "Only—"

"That horse can't be ridden, Dwyer?"

"I think not, but—"

"Would you give it to a man who could ride it?"

"I suppose so—" began Barney, "but—"

"You wanted to see Len Peary. You'll have a chance. You'll have a chance to see him move, too. Peary!"

It was as though he had set a bugle to his lips and blown a blast. And far away a door was heard to slam, and footfalls came racing—footfalls as soft as the padded step of a cat, and coming toward them as swiftly as a great cat can run!

6

A door flashed open in the side of the room, and that pantherlike youth, Leonard Peary, sprang in with a revolver in his hand. He straightened from a crouching position, gradually.

"I thought you yelled—" he said to Big Mack.

"I wanted you fast, but I don't need your gun." said McGregor. "Here's the fellow you handed five phony dollars to."

Young Peary put up his gun, strode to Barney, and stared him in the eye.

"What have you got to say about it?" he demanded. "I've heard that you can break men in two. What have you got to say to me?"

His fearlessness and his contempt made him a fine picture that Barney was able to admire so heartily that he merely smiled and shook his head.

"I wouldn't fight you for five dollars," said Barney. "Fighting you would be a bad business, I think."

Big Mack began to laugh softly. Peary, after staring at Barney for another instant, turned on his heel toward McGregor.

"Is he trying to make a fool of me? Is he trying to talk down to me, Mack?" he demanded.

"If you owe him five dollars, give it to him," said McGregor.

Peary, without turning, flung a gold piece on the floor. It rolled into a corner, and Barney humbly pursued and captured it.

Peary was exclaiming: "You can't make a monkey out of me, Mack!"

"Don't be a fool," said McGregor. "You're wanting a real horse, you've said? Well, look at that red mare out the window. She's yours if you can ride her. Go take a try. If you can't handle her, nobody can."

Peary went to the window and looked at the mare. He whistled.

"I'll ride her or take the hide off her!" he said, and was instantly outside the room.

Big Mack had finished his meal. Now he came to the window with another tumbler of whiskey and looked out on the contest, while Barney Dwyer stood at his side, feeling that he had been tricked into venturing the mare in such a chance, knowing that whether he could ride her or not, she had more value to him than any other horse in the world.

Leonard Peary went out and stood by the mare, while he tightened his belt. Then he whipped into the saddle with a yell and threw the quirt into the horse. There was no second stroke of that whip. The mare rose like a cloud of fire; she dropped again like a thunderbolt. The earth was furnished with springs, casting her up higher and higher. At last she spun on the ground like a wheel and slung Peary skidding along the ground.

He was up at once.

"Thirty seconds, Len," said McGregor, from the window. Pure joy made Barney laugh, though he was sure that laughter was dangerous.

Peary was perfectly at ease, however. He dusted himself off, arranged his bandana at his throat, and took note of a tear in his trousers.

"I know why you laugh," he said, nodding at Barney. "You taught her to buck, eh?"

"No," said Barney. "I haven't taught her."

"You lie," stated Peary, though still without heat. "You trained her."

"Don't call people liars. Not while they're in my house," said Big Mack coldly.

"It's not your house. It's Bunny Walsh's house. And this fellow trained her, all right. Did you see her start off fence-rowing? She switched to sun-fishing, and finished me off with a spin. She's an educated devil, Mack. You could see for yourself."

"Going to try her again?" asked McGregor.

"Of course I am," said Peary. "I'll ride her, too!"

The fear leaped up in the heart of Barney Dwyer.

"No," he called. "Once is enough. That's all I agreed to! One try is enough, and she won!"

"You won't let me try her again?" asked Peary.

"Sorry," said Barney. "She means a lot to me. She's like a friend! Come here, girl!"

He held out his hand, but as she started to come to him, Peary caught the rein and checked her.

"Let me see you try to stop me!" exclaimed Peary. "I'm going to ride her or bust. You stop me if you can!"

The mare pulled back on the reins, snorting, backing to reach her master at the window, and at the sight of her effort to come to him, Barney felt a prickling of gooseflesh all over his skin and a burning heat inside him. He laid his hand on the sill of the window, ready to leap down on the outside.

"Let go of her, Peary!" he called.

"I'm damned if I do," answered Peary.

"Let her go," commanded Big Mack. "She belongs to Barney Dwyer, here just now! Let her alone, Len!"

Peary, gradually relaxing his grip on the rein, obeyed that order, but his dark eyes were fixed not on McGregor but on Barney Dwyer.

"We'll see some more of each other, Dwyer!" he said.

"Of course you will, Len," declared Big Mack. "Come in here. We'll have a chat with Dwyer, the two of us."

Leonard Peary returned to the room, flung himself into a chair, and lounged back in it with his legs stretched out. He was scowling.

"What's there to talk about?" asked Peary. "Doesn't seem to me that *talking* is in place now!"

McGregor, carrying his half-finished whiskey back to the table, took his former place and sipped the drink.

"I'll decide when it's time to stop talking," he declared. "Dwyer, come out with it. What's your game? What brought you up here? Who are you?"

Barney moistened his lips. He could feel that he had come to a crisis, and that slow brain of his refused to furnish him with words for an answer.

"I'm John McGregor. You know that. This is Len Peary. You know that, too. Now, we want to know who Barney Dwyer is. Let's have the news!"

"I'm just a ranch hand," said Barney. "I came up here from the Peary ranch to collect five dollars that Daniel Peary still owed me. He told me to get it from his son. He told me to bring his son back with me."

The two others stared at him.

"This stuff about taking Peary home to the ranch. What sort of rot is that?" asked McGregor.

He held the whiskey glass at his lips, waiting for the answer before he drank.

"You see how it is," explained Barney. "His father is getting older, I guess. He wants his son back home. He doesn't like having him in Timberline. He told me that he'd like it a lot if I brought him back home."

"How would you take him, Dwyer?" asked Big Mack.

Barney looked down at his hands.

"Well, I'd just bring him along, I suppose," said he.

"Just tie you on behind his saddle, Len," said McGregor to Peary. "That's all he'd do. Take you along with him like a blanket roll!"

He smiled a little.

"Are you going to let him talk this sort of bunk and get away with it?" asked Peary.

"No," answered McGregor. "I won't let him get away with it. Dwyer, who have you talked to in Timberline?"

"Why, just to you two, and a bartender, and Riley Quintin,

and Susan Jones, and Wash, and a boy, and the sheriff," said Barney.

"You talked to the sheriff? What did he have to say?"

"He thought that I was one of you, one of your men, McGregor. He told me that he was going to clear up everything and everybody. He said that he'd do it, or die. He said that the men before him had been murdered or bought off, and that he wouldn't be bought, and that he would take a good deal of killing. That's about what he said."

McGregor studied him. Then he said: "Did the sheriff say anything particular about Peary?"

"No."

"Didn't say that he specially wanted him?"

"No."

McGregor looked significantly toward Peary, and the latter nodded and smiled faintly with pleasure.

"You won't talk out to me, Dwyer?" asked McGregor. "You won't come clean with me?"

"I've said everything. I've told you the whole truth," said Barney Dwyer.

McGregor stood up and raised a finger. Len Peary unsheathed a pair of guns and directed the muzzles carelessly toward Barney, without rising from his chair.

"That's right, keep him covered," said McGregor. "Don't you know enough to hoist your hands, Dwyer?"

"Yes!" exclaimed Barney and stretched his arms so violently above his head that the gesture brought him on tiptoe

"He thinks he'll get a laugh with this low comedy work," said Peary. "Watch him, chief. I've got an idea that he's poison, and a new kind of poison, at that!"

McGregor stepped back from searching Barney.

"He's a new kind, all right," said he, juggling a pocket-knife that he had taken from Barney Dwyer. "No gun. Only this to cut his way through the world. He just about beats me, Len. Get a pair of those handcuffs that Sheriff Cary loaned us last year. Maybe Dwyer's nerve will rust faster than the steel of those handcuffs. We'll make a try of it, and see!"

7

They took Barney Dwyer back through a kitchen, where the smell of food was a torment to him. Old Wash, in the act of putting a big pan of bread into the oven, looked up at the three, saw the manacled hands of Barney Dwyer, and glanced hastily down again.

Peary opened in the floor a cellar door. McGregor took a lantern from the wall and went first, lighting the way down a flight of damp stone steps into a room piled with provisions. Beyond this was a still larger room, three walls of which were stone. The fourth wall, into which the door was let, was rough masonry, big, rounded stones cemented together to make the partition. One pillar of the natural rock had been left in the center of the room to uphold the floor of the house above. It was the storage place of wood. Some good-sized pieces were corded along one side of the chamber.

"Think of Bunny going to all the trouble of having this place dug out!" said Peary. "What did he think he'd put here? Treasure?"

"He's romantic," answered McGregor. "That's why I like him. Now look here, Dwyer. You can see that there's no way for you out of this room. You stay here and think things over. We'll look in on you tomorrow, maybe, and see if you feel more like talking."

"I'll talk now!" cried Barney desperately. "You wouldn't leave me here in the dark, would you? I'll talk now!"

McGregor lifted the lantern until the light of it flashed in the eyes of Barney.

"We've all got our little weaknesses," sneered McGregor. "What broke your nerve about darkness, Dwyer? Ever do a stretch of solitary in the pen? Well, if you'll talk, come out

34

with it. I've guessed part of the truth already, I think. Dutch Hendry is working with you. Dutch sent you up here to drop a monkey wrench into my machine. Is that it?''

"No," exclaimed Barney. "I've never even heard of Dutch Hendry. I've told you the whole truth. I'll tell you more of it. I'll tell you everything that ever happened in my life and—''

"You've been telling me the truth, have you?" said McGregor. "Well, then you stay here till you can think up some interesting lies. Sorry the floor's a little wet. But you can sleep dry enough, on that woodpile. So long!''

He went out; the door slammed; the lock turned with a grinding, a rusty clank of iron against iron; then the terrible velvet blackness fell upon the eyes and across the brain of Barney Dwyer.

He dropped to his knees and gripped his hair with both hands. The darkness of a shut room had been a horror to him ever since his childhood.

They would look in tomorrow—perhaps! Twenty-four hours of this would bring madness to him, he thought.

He found the woodpile and leaned against it, gripping the rough wood, breathing the resinous fragrance of the pine. And that restored him.

He found the door and leaned his weight against it, but the door held. He had known it would hold. The ponderous clang of it in shutting had told him that he would not be able to break the lock.

He went to the corner of the room and fumbled until he found a stone much larger than its neighbors in the wall. He scratched the cement and felt it come away in small flakes under the tips of his fingers.

So, not with hope, but because he felt that inaction would drive him insane, he wedged his shoulders against the corner of the adjoining wall and stamped his feet against the face of that larger stone in the masonry. With pulsing efforts, he thrust out.

He thought his feet had merely slipped on the smooth surface, at first, but then he heard a faint noise of something falling. He thrust again, and then the stone was dislodged. He heard it bump heavily on the other side of the wall, against the floor of the provision room.

The hole was large, and he quickly made it larger, pulling out adjoining bits of rocks from the mortar that embedded them, until he was able to wriggle through the opening. He lay still for a moment, panting, incredulous of this escape.

He stood up to fumble for the stairs, and as he felt his way through the darkness, he heard a rasping noise. A wedge of light from the stairs struck his feet, spilling across the floor. It jerked upward and steadied on his face. It was a dark lantern that had just been unshuttered.

The voice of Len Peary said: "You were right, chief. I don't know how he managed it, but there he is. Look at that hole in the wall."

"He's silent dynamite," said Big Mack. "He explodes but he doesn't make a noise. Bring in a fifth-chain from the wagon shed, will you?"

"I'll have it here in a jiffy," said Peary, running up the stairs. "But how did he get through that wall? Did he gnaw it open?"

The door opened and slammed at the head of the stairs.

"Well done, Dwyer," said McGregor, coming down to the foot of the steps. "How did you get through that wall?"

He used the lantern to examine the breach.

"I pushed through," said Barney, rather feebly. "I wedged my back against the other wall in the corner, and I pushed through."

"I believe it," said McGregor.

He came up to Barney, put the muzzle of a revolver against the breast of his prisoner, and then, with the hand that also held the lantern, fingered the shoulder of Barney, working the tips of his fingers among the big rubbery fibers.

"You're not so big, Dwyer," said he. "Not more than two hundred pounds, I'd say. But strength isn't a matter of poundage, with some people. Two hundred pounds of wildcat, for instance, would go a long way."

He had the air of a jockey looking over a fine horse.

"I could use you, Dwyer. The way you keep your face is a charm, to me. I'll tell you what—for a time I was on the

verge of breaking down. For a while I was about ready to
believe that you were actually no more than a simple ranch·
hand—an extra simple one with simply an extra share of
strength in your hands. But there was a flicker of something
else in you. I could feel the heat even when I couldn't see the
flame. I knew that there was a fire in you, somehow. That
was why we came back here to watch for a little while. I
heard the door groan and shudder and knew you were at it.
And it gave me a groan and a shudder, too, Dwyer, to think
what would happen if you got those paws of yours on me."

He stepped back a little, and again threw the flare of the
lantern's light straight against the eyes of Barney Dwyer, who
steadied his glance a little, seeing the wavering image of the
flame in the brightness of the polished reflector, inside.

This seemed to be of importance to Big Mack, who
muttered, partly to himself: "You could look right into the
eye of the sun, too, I suppose?"

Still Barney Dwyer did not speak. Words were evolving
slowly in the back of his mind, but they would not reach his
lips. He felt that a steer might wait in this manner for the
butcher's mallet to fall.

Young Leonard Peary returned, carrying a heavy weight of
chain on which eight horses could safely pull. The door was
unlocked once more. McGregor passed the big fifth-chain
around the slender steel links that bound the wrists of Barney
together. Then he put the chain around the pillar and padlocked
it together. He stepped back and played the light of the
lantern over the picture before he left it.

He asked: "How does it look to you, Len?"

"That'll hold a plough team. It ought to hold a man," said
Peary.

"Yes, it ought to hold him," agreed McGregor.

He stepped up to his prisoner, saying: "Wait outside for
me, Len."

Peary passed into the provision room, and McGregor said
very quietly: "Now, Dwyer, you see how it is. You have no
chance. I've got you, and I'm going to keep you. However,
I'm not a fool. I know how to value a man when I find one.
Talk straight to me and you'll find that I'm open to reason.

Probably you could make more, working for me, than you
ever have made working alone. Perhaps Dutch Hendry isn't
behind you. Perhaps you're working your game alone. But
whatever it is, you can understand that I'd be committing
suicide if I let a fellow like you run loose in my part of the
country. There isn't room in the whole of the Rocky Mountains for two men like you and me! Come, now. Will you
talk?''

And he flashed his lantern again into the eyes of Barney
Dwyer.

Desperately, Barney strove to think of a lie that would fill
the imagination of even a McGregor. He could say that he
was a bank robber, or a train robber. He could say that a life
of crime stretched behind him, but how could he convince
McGregor without sufficient details? How could he really
offer an explanation of a purpose sufficient to bring him into
these mountains?

Before he was half-ready to speak, McGregor snarled: "All
right, Dwyer. It's to be a contest of strength, eh? Well, man,
I tell you I'll keep you here till the handcuffs rust off your
wrists. I'll starve you, damn you, or else I'll get words out of
you.''

He left and slammed the door, and the darkness swallowed
Barney again. He heard the footfalls go up the stairs. He
heard the sharp, rapid voice of McGregor speaking to Peary
until the second door shut this noise away.

Then, at last, a sound bubbled up in the throat of Barney
Dwyer. Even that groan died before it reached his teeth.

He leaned his forehead against the damp coldness of the
stone. There was no hope. There was no thought of hope,
unless he could break the chain that bound his wrists together.

He put his feet against the base of the column of natural
rock, swayed back, and gave his mighty strength to the pull.
The handcuffs turned into collars of fire on his wrists; but the
chain held!

A pull would not turn the trick. A sudden wrench with all
his force might give him a better chance. It might, also, crush
all the bones in his wrists and hands. But even to be handless

for life would be better than to die here, in the gravelike darkness of the cellar.

He turned his hands into two bulging fists, the better to cushion the shock. He replanted his feet at the base of the pillar. Then he swayed his weight far back, thrusting with the power of his legs, jerking with the strength of back and shoulders and arms.

The chain parted. The impetus of his lunge skated him far off along the cellar floor.

He got to his knees and remained there a moment with his head thrown back, trying to give thanks. But not a word entered his mind. Blood dripped from the fingers of his left hand. While the red was still running, he wanted to fasten his clutch on the throat of McGregor. That was the image that filled his mind, instead of prayer—his grip on the throat of McGregor, and Big Mack on his knees, biting like a frantic, helpless dog at the wrists that still wore the steel bracelets.

Then Barney stood up, found the hole in the wall, and squirmed through it a second time. There would be no third imprisonment. He knew that. If he had to use his naked hands against guns, still he would not surrender to them again.

He stole noiselessly up the stairs.

8

At the door above, he bowed and listened for his life. He heard footfalls crossing the kitchen, treading on the cellar trap and knocking dust into the face of Barney. The step went on. Another door closed lightly. Might it not mean that Wash had left the kitchen?

No better chance seemed likely to come, at any rate. So Barney lifted one wing of the trap door and looked cautiously out.

The room was empty!

Stealthily he crawled out. The back door was open on the dark of the night. Beyond the other door he could hear the voice of McGregor saying: "If you want the girl, Peary, you don't want your place with me. I won't give my confidence to any man who's tied to apron strings."

"Then sooner or later I'll have to break with you. I'll have to break anyway, if I hope to get her. She's told me that," said the voice of Peary. "She knows that I'm hand in glove with you, Mack. And she hates the idea. Stolen money is poison to her."

"All right," said McGregor. "Do as you please. Only give me warning. And this is the last that I want to hear about Sue Jones or any other girl that comes into your life. Women are a waste of time."

The voice of Peary began to answer, but the words had no meaning to Barney. He was too occupied with stealing across that floor without permitting the boards to creak, putting down his feet cautiously, the outer edge first. Yet, reaching the table, he could not avoid stretching out his hand and passing a package of raisins into his pocket.

As he did so, a door creaked, the voice of Peary entered suddenly into the room, saying: "Wilson told me about the tunnel that they cut under the wall. Wait a minute and I'll tell you what he said—"

For at the door between the kitchen and the dining room stood Leonard Peary, pushing it open, still talking with his head turned toward McGregor.

It was impossible for Barney to get suddenly from the room without betraying himself with the noise he made. Therefore he stole straight at Peary, and as the latter stepped on into the kitchen, he turned his head just in time to have a bleeding fist clip him on the chin.

With wide-open eyes, Peary stared at Barney, but they were the eyes of a sleepwalker. The second blow which Barney had started, he checked in midair and, instead, caught up the sagging body lest it should slump noisily to the floor.

Not till he had the weight of Peary in his arms did he remember the greater purpose that had been in his mind when he came to Timberline.

So, holding his breath, the head, the arms, and the legs of Peary trailing down from his grasp, he crossed the kitchen floor.

"Hurry it up, Peary!" called the loud voice of McGregor. "Bring the coffee with you, too."

Barney with his burden reached the outer door. The boards of the veranda creaked ominously under his tread. He got to the ground with a leap, and then ran hard toward the barn that stood behind the house.

There was only the dimmest twilight to show it to him, but there he would have to get transportation for Peary and himself. There, surely, they must have placed the red mare!

As he pulled open the nearest door of the barn, Peary stirred, groaned, began to struggle.

That meant further delay when every moment was a breath of life to him. At least, in "fanning" him, McGregor had not taken the twine from his pocket. He used a length of it now to tie the hands of Peary behind his back.

One of the row of stalled horses began to whinny loudly, and Barney knew that sound as well as though it were a human voice. It was the red mare, calling to him, betraying him with her love.

He groaned at the ear of Peary: "Stop trying to break away. I've got you. Keep in front of me. If you yell, I'll strangle you, Peary!"

In the meantime, he was picking saddle, bridle, and blanket from the peg on which they hung. And Peary obediently stood close by while the first horse was saddled. It was a gray, whose bright color made it easier to work on her in the almost total darkness of the barn. The next in order was a taller horse; Dwyer jerked saddle and bridle on this one, also.

The voice of Peary kept gasping and muttering: "Dwyer, don't do it! Don't take me away like a chicken picked out of a henhouse. I'd rather be murdered. The whole range will start laughing at me. I'll be shamed, Dwyer. For God's sake, give me a fair chance! I'll do anything you want. I don't care what your game is, I'll play into your hands. But to be kidnapped like a baby—"

"Be still!" said Barney Dwyer. "Come with me down here while I get the mare!"

She was in a frenzy of excitement, rearing, stamping, pulling back on the rope that tethered her to the manger. But when Barney came near, she was quiet at once, her whinny no more than a whisper of greeting.

He sighed with happiness as his hand touched the silk of her flank. That battered saddle that Daniel Peary had given with her was quickly on her back and the bridle over her head. He led her to the first two horses and untied their lead ropes. He was at the door of the barn, with Peary beside him, when the great voice of McGregor rang through the night: "Peary! Len Peary! What's come of you, man?"

Instantly the cry of Peary answered, pitched wild and high by desperation: "Here! Quick, Mack! The devil's got me helpless in his hands. Dwyer—"

The grip of Barney strangled that shouting voice.

He picked up the struggling bulk of Peary like a sack of bran, threw it across the saddle of the gray horse, and himself sprang onto the back of the tall gelding, which had been second in the line.

With the grip of his knees he had to hold his place. With one hand he guided the gray. With the other hand, he mastered Peary and kept him in place, while the horses broke into a trot.

A glance to the side showed a dim figure racing from the house. A gun spoke, sending the whir of a bullet high above his head.

"He's on the left horse!" yelled the voice of Peary. "Stop him, Mack! I'm tied! I'm tied!"

The gun spoke again, and this time the shot cut close to Barney's head.

He swung the horses clumsily around the end of a haystack and brought them to a gallop, while the red mare ranged ahead, dancing, leaping, pitching in her joy of freedom and of motion.

Side by side the horses cantered.

"You'll have no good of it in the end!" groaned Peary. "You may win today, but before the finish you'll be cursing. I'm going to kill you for this, Dwyer. I'm going to kill you inch by inch!"

But Barney was too busy to answer. He was tying another
length of twine that passed from the wrists of Leonard Peary
across his body and was fastened at the other end to the horn
of the saddle. After that, and only now, he remembered
weapons. Under each of Peary's armpits he found a revolver
held by a spring holster. These he transferred to the two
empty holsters that were attached to the saddle in which he
was himself sitting. Last, he fastened the reins to the pommel
of his saddle, and now he was ready for riding at full speed.

The horses, unguided, had slanted across to the trail that
pointed toward the town of Timberline, whose lights were
scattered in irregular groupings before them; now Barney
urged them to a full gallop down that road. Perhaps Big Mack
was already on the road, rushing in pursuit.

"D'you hear me?" shouted Peary. "If you try to take me
into Timberline, if you let the people see me tied up like a
bundle of laundry I'll throw myself off the horse. There'll be
nothing but a dead rag of me, and be damned to you!"

"Where else can I take you?" called Barney in answer.

"There's a draw to the left that you can ride down. D'you
see it now?" urged Peary. "Turn down it! He'll never guess
you've gone that way around the town!"

It opened like a wide, shallow trench, and into it rode
Barney, for he knew that his captive was desperated enough
to commit suicide rather than allow himself to be made into a
public spectacle.

Thick turf muffled the beating hoofs of their horses, and so
he was able to hear the ringing gallop of the pursuer, flying
straight down the trail toward Timberline.

9

If that was Big Mack, his horse kept on raising the echoes all
the way into Timberline, while Barney, beginning to breathe
again, put the horses into a trot.

They went steadily on out of the big hollow in which the town stood. From the brim of the slope, Barney looked back on the lights of Timberline and so passed on among the hills until the darkness of the forest began around him. He had not the slightest idea of his place or of the proper direction.

So at last he said to his companion: "Peary, can you tell me the way back to your father's ranch?"

A rage of groaning and of curses broke from the lips of Peary. "What'll you gain by that?" he demanded. "D'you mean to say that my father offered you enough coin to make it worth your while to risk your neck taking me back home?"

"No, not for your father, so much."

"For what, then?"

"Sue Jones thinks you ought to go home," said Barney.

"I'm going crazy!" exclaimed Len Peary. "*She* thinks that I ought to go home? You want her. She says that you can have her once I'm brushed out of the way. So you cart me away like a watchdog that's a nuisance. Dwyer, when I first saw your smooth mug, I thought that I'd have the killing of you, someday, and enjoy it. Now I know that I will!"

"Have her?" cried Barney. "D'you think that she'd so much as look at a simple fellow, like me?"

"A simple fellow like you, eh? So simple that you make a fool of McGregor and take me off under your arm like a bit of firewood? So simple that you walk through Timberline, scaring the town to death? You *are* a fool, though, if you think that other people can't see through all your pretending. But Sue—oh God! She's through with me and she's told you to get me out of the way."

Such a helpless fury came over Barney that he leaned from his saddle and struck Peary across the mouth with the back of his hand.

Peary gasped and reeled.

"Keep the dirty talk off your tongue and out of your throat!" said Barney in such a voice as never had issued before from his lips. "Or else I'll—"

He stopped himself before the last words were spoken. But he knew what he had intended to say, and that intention shocked him. He was ashamed of the blow he had struck a helpless man.

In the meantime, he could not ride on blindly, perhaps going in exactly the wrong direction. So he made a halt in a glade beneath the trees that was like a great hall, with the brown trunks for pillars, and the green of the spreading branches for a roof.

There he unsaddled and tethered the two horses; lashed the right arm of Peary to his left arm, kicked the pine needles into a deep bed, and lay down.

He had not spoken to Peary since he struck the blow. And Peary attempted no speech on his side. In silence, Barney lay for a moment, staring up at the darkness. He fell asleep.

The squirrels wakened him. Profound gloom covered the lower stretches of the forest, still, but the gray of the morning had reached the higher branches, and the nut-gatherers were chattering.

Barney turned his head and looked into the dark eyes of young Peary, brilliant with hatred. That was the way they began the second day.

He shared the last of the raisins with his captive, then saddled and bridled the horses and took an upward slope that brought them out of the trees on the high shoulder of a mountain. From that point, he took his bearings, located in the distances the flashing face of the water that had been his guide toward Timberline, and struck out in this direction.

The mare still followed, or ran ahead, or came back to prance at the side of her master, or raced off until trees or hummocks concealed her.

She was such a beauty as she frolicked, that Peary watched her with a hungry eye. Now the mare flashed into view with a loud neigh and fled as if for her life toward them. She had come in this manner before, however, except that her ears had never been flattened quite so close to her neck.

"Is there something in that wood?" asked Barney, only half aloud.

"She saw a shadow, that's all," answered Peary. "When a

horse or a man starts in making a fool of itself, it enjoys jumping when it sees even the wind in the grass!"

The mare cast a rapid loop around them and halted in the rear, whinnying again, like a trumpet call.

"There's something wrong," said Barney. "She means something by that."

"You know horse language, eh?" sneered Peary.

His upper lip was swollen and empurpled by the blow that it had received the night before; his whole mouth twisted a little to the side as he stared in contempt at Barney.

"She's calling us back!" insisted Barney, staring at the green shadows of the wood as he came up to it. They were close to it now, and he drew rein, halting both horses.

"Maybe she sees a ghost!" said Peary in scorn.

And as he spoke, out from under the branches of the trees rode four men, each with a rifle balanced across the pommel of the saddle. And he who was in the lead was none other than the sheriff, who had spoken to Barney the evening before.

It was far too late to cut the twine that tied Peary and Barney Dwyer together and then to flee. With a twitch of his fingers, Barney snapped that tough, hard-twisted cord, but the four, fanning out into a wide semicircle, were close on them.

"It's Jim Elder!" groaned Peary. "Don't try to run. He doesn't know how to miss with a rifle. I don't know what game you were trying to play, Dwyer, but he's going to finish it for you! Damn you, you've sewed me up in a sack and made me a present to him. You knew he wanted me!"

The sheriff shifted his rifle until he was carrying it at the ready. Close by, he spoke to his horse and halted it.

"Something told me that I'd find you again, Dwyer," said he. "And I even guessed the sort of company that you'd be in. But how do your hands happen to be tied, Peary?"

Peary took a great breath and said nothing. He was white with shame.

"Get behind 'em, Mike," said the sheriff to one of his men. "Mind you, if you see any queer moves, don't stop to ask for orders, but shoot, and shoot to kill."

"I'm only achin' for the chance," answered Mike. "I won't need telling to take my share out of 'em."

"Get off those horses!" commanded the sheriff. "Pete and Harry, fan 'em. Get everything down to the skin."

"Are you aiming to arrest me, Sheriff Elder?" asked Peary.

"I'm aiming to arrest you; and I'm aiming to hang you, too, when the time comes," said the sheriff.

Peary, dismounting clumsily because of his tied hands, answered: "You can't arrest me without a charge!"

"I would have arrested you any time the last three months, without a charge," declared the sheriff. "I would have arrested you and taken my chance of digging up the right sort of evidence, once I had a grip on you. But now I've got you and the evidence, all at once. You're a slippery lad, Peary, but I think that a good hemp rope could be fitted to your neck tight enough to stay!"

"What's the charge?" asked Peary, firmly enough.

"Robbery and murder," said the sheriff.

"It's a faked lot of evidence that you have, then!" said Peary.

"You never killed a man, eh, boy?" asked the sheriff.

"Not unless it was self-defense!"

"You stuck up the Coffeeville stage last week, and you killed Buddy Marsh on the driver's seat," said the sheriff.

At that, a big fellow who was searching Peary grabbed him by the lapels of the coat and shook him violently, while he yelled at the top of his voice: "And you're gunna hang for it. You're gunna hang for it by the law, or by me!"

"Steady, Pete, steady," said the sheriff. "He'll hang for it, all right, without any help from you. We've got the evidence on you, Peary!"

"You bought it, and you bought a lie, then!" cried Peary.

"That may all be true," said the sheriff. "We have judges and juries to find out the truth of things. Our job is just to find the bloodsuckers and bring them in when we can!"

He turned on Dwyer.

"Now, who are you?" he asked.

"I'm Barney Dwyer. I was working on the Peary ranch. I was fired. But Daniel Peary told me that if I could bring back his son, he'd be glad to see me again. I came up here. I found Peary. He and McGregor thought there was something strange about me. They shut me into the cellar and put handcuffs on me. They were going to starve me until I confessed what had brought me up to Timberline. I managed to get away, took Peary and a couple of horses from the barn, and got this far, when I met you."

"They put you in handcuffs in the cellar, eh?" said the sheriff. "How did you get away?"

"First I kicked a hole in the wall and got out, but they put me back in again—"

"That's a heavy stone wall up yonder in the cellar of Bunny's house," put in Mike.

"I don't expect anyone to believe me," said Barney. "But I'm telling you because you asked. The second time, they chained me to the stone post in the center of the room, so I broke the chain of the handcuffs and crawled out, and got Peary and came away, just as I've told you."

"I think you can rest in jail with the story for a while," said the sheriff. "Any proofs of that yarn?"

"The hole is still there in the cellar wall, I suppose," said Barney. "And here are the handcuffs still on my wrists."

The sheriff gave a faint grunt of surprise. He stepped forward and examined the steel bracelets that still covered the wrists of Barney, the dangling links of the steel chain being tucked inside the metal circlets. The mere stretching forward of Barney's arms caused the cuffs of his sleeves to rise and expose the handcuffs. The wrists were chafed. The backs of the hands were swollen and discolored.

The sheriff stepped back again and shook his head.

"That pair of hands looks as though you were telling the truth," he said. "But that's a new steel chain. No man could snap it the way you say you have. It would hold a horse. Besides, your whole story is a funny thing to listen to. Did Daniel Peary offer you a lot of money to bring back Len Peary?"

"No," said Barney.

"Do you expect me to believe you?"

"No," repeated Barney. "It's the truth, but nobody would believe it, I suppose."

Two or three of the men guffawed at this, but the sheriff stepped a little closer.

"It's a queer tale, Dwyer," said he. "Down in my heart, I think that you're a thug. But you brought me Len Peary with his hands tied, and that may have saved some bloodletting all around. Besides, I haven't anything against you. To do what you say you've done, you'd have to have the strength of a horse. Can you show me some of that strength, Dwyer?"

"I've heard of a strong man that could bend a horseshoe," said Mike. "Wait a minute. I've got the shoe that my horse cast this mornin'. Let him try to bend that one!"

He chuckled as he spoke, and hurrying to his horse, he brought from the saddlebag a quite new horseshoe, the iron thick for wear on the mountain rocks.

Barney took it in his hands and made an effort. He merely hurt his fingers, and stopped a moment to look down at the insides of them where the flesh was bruised.

"He's a fake," said Mike. "You bring him along, Elder!"

Once more, Barney put his hands on the heavy semicircle. All the twisting strength of his hands came into play. His forearms swelled until the sleeves of his shirt were filled solidly. There was a faint cracking sound, then a distinct snap.

"I'm sorry," said Barney. "I guess I've spoiled that horseshoe."

And he held out the two broken fragments to Mike.

A more than churchly silence fell over that group. Mike received the broken horseshoe with both hands, reverently.

"It must of had a flaw," said Pete, leaning nearer.

"No," muttered Mike. "Look for yourself. That's a clean break in good iron. Doggone my eyes!"

He lifted those eyes toward Barney, slowly shaking his head. As for the sheriff, he was supporting his chin with one hand while he considered Barney Dwyer, but finally he said: "Perhaps I'm wrong. But I'm going to believe you, Dwyer. Let me try my keys on those handcuffs, if you wish."

He took out a small batch of them, studied the locks of the manacles, and at the second try he made the wrists of Barney free. After that, he mounted his men, with Leonard Peary among them.

And he said briefly: "Perhaps I ought to pick you up as a horse thief, Dwyer, because you've admitted taking two horses from McGregor. But things taken from McGregor don't mean exactly stolen, to me. That red mare ought to do you for any riding you have ahead. So long, and all the luck you deserve!"

But Peary, as they rode off together, turned his head, and looked with fixed, bright hatred toward Barney Dwyer. A dip of the ground and a bending of the trail took them presently out of sight.

10

Barney Dwyer sat on a rock by the edge of the bright, flowing water. He had failed, and now his heart was empty, and all the beauty of that mountain valley seemed to him an empty thing, too.

He had failed, and yet if he had trusted the mare and his own instincts, he would not have allowed Peary to fall into the sheriff's hands! He would have been warned in time to turn far aside and flee from that danger.

It was Leonard Peary who had laughed him out of his proper intention. They were wise, all these other people, all these other cunning, tricky men. And yet sometimes they made mistakes. Sometimes simplicity could see deeper and farther into the truth, it appeared.

He was brooding on this, when he heard the rattling of hoofs coming down the trail. He remembered Big Mack as he heard the sound, and suddenly was aware that once more he was unarmed.

So he started up, and the red mare came to him as though she, also, knew that danger was rushing toward them. Beside him, she faced about, snorting and stamping. Oh, if he could sit the saddle on her, he could laugh at all riders in the world, he felt! He could leave them as though he wore wings that could carry him smoothly and swiftly over the mountains!

The approaching horseman was out of sight, beyond the trees, the hoofbeats grew louder, and suddenly it was Susan Jones on a racing pinto pony that swept down on Barney. The tan collar of her blouse flew in her face; the brim of her sombrero curled with the speed of her going.

When she saw Barney, she turned suddenly aside and drew rein. The pebbles scattered and rattled far before her as the hoofs of the mustang slid to a halt.

"Have you seen Len Peary? Has he been down this trail?" she called out.

"Yes," said Barney, sadly.

"Which way?" she exclaimed. She was wild with excitement. Her face was flushed. The bigness of her eyes made her look like a child.

"Did he go down the trail, or up? Did he—"

"That way," said Barney, pointing across country. And all the time his heart was aching. For how many men have such women been in such agonies of fear? But there was no other woman like her, and never would be.

"That way? That side trail?" she repeated eagerly. "Thank heavens! The sheriff—he was going to block this trail. I couldn't find Len to warn him if he happened to come down this way."

Suddenly she was grave again, staring into the upturned misery of his face.

"What's the matter?" she asked.

He pointed toward the empty side trail for a moment before he could speak.

"The sheriff has him," he said.

She slid from the horse as though all the strength had run out of her body. He looked at her pale, compressed lips, and tried to turn himself into steel so that he could speak.

"We ran straight into them. Right straight into them," he said.

"Were you with him, then?" cried the girl, "Is Len hurt?"

"There wasn't any fighting; Peary's hands were tied," said Barney. "I—I tied them," he ended feebly, explaining: "There wasn't any other way to bring him from Timberline. He's too dangerous to leave with his hand free. He didn't want to come away with me, you see."

She struck both her hands against her face, then cried: "What happened? *What* happened?"

"I got him at McGregor's house and carried him away, with a pair of McGregor's horses. I lost the way and had to sleep in the woods, with Peary tied to me. Then we came down here—and the sheriff and some other men came suddenly out at us with rifles. And Peary's hands were tied, you see?"

"Are you telling me that you, alone, were taking him away?" she asked.

"You wanted him gone. You told me you wanted him away from Timberline and back on his ranch," said Barney. "I don't think that I ever would have touched him, except that you said that."

"And the sheriff—" groaned the girl. "God help me! Poor Len! You—you—you took him away with his hands tied? Are you mad? Are you a half-wit? Are you a simpleton? Why do you stand there speechless and goggle at me?"

Every word struck Barney to the heart.

"I'm not very clever," he said. "I was trying to do what you wanted me to do."

She caught him by the thick round of his wrists, and shook his arms.

"Is this still the same play acting?" she demanded. "Have you told me the truth? What—"

She seemed to feel for the first time the heat of his swollen wrists, and snatching away her hands, she looked at the bruised hands that had seemed so helpless in her grasp. From them she looked up into that grief-stricken face.

"I'm going to be patient," said the girl. "Will you tell me what happened, all of it?"

"I've told you. They had me in handcuffs, Peary and McGregor. They thought that I was something important. They were going to starve me into saying what I was. But I'm nothing. There was nothing to confess, except what you've seen just now: that I'm not very clever. I'm not as bright as other people."

He flushed miserably. "I managed to get away and take Peary with me," he said. "I was trying to please you. I didn't know that the sheriff would be here."

His voice trailed away. He seemed to be waiting for her to strike him. And into her bright eyes there rushed a sudden understanding that was like a shadow. She drew back from him a little, murmuring: "Oh! It's really that!" He felt her judging him, pitying him; he felt scorn and anger and disgust, all combined.

But he must give to her the entire bitterness of the truth. He said: "The sheriff charged Peary with holding up the Coffeeville stage and killing Buddy Marsh, the driver."

She got hold of the reins of her pinto, close to the bit, and steadied herself with that support.

"I'd rather be dead than see you look all white and sick!" cried Barney suddenly. "I'll tell you what I'll do. I'll go after them. I'll try to get Peary free again."

"Hush!" said the girl. "Do you think that I can let you throw yourself away? You've tried to do what's best. You've done all you could—for me!"

One sob rippled up her throat and broke from her lips. But not a tear fell. She mastered herself at once.

"What could *you* do against all of them? No, no, I've got to find Big Mack. *He'll* manage something. But oh, the life of a man like Leonard Peary thrown away by the blundering of a—"

Fury sparkled in her eyes for an instant. Then she swung lightly into the saddle and darted back up the trail. She left Barney standing with his head bent, his arms swinging a little forward, helplessly, like those of a man exhausted by the lifting of great burdens.

She had said, in effect: "Oh, to think of the life of a man like Leonard Peary thrown away by a half-wit, a simpleton, a worthless fool!"

He looked down the trail along which the sheriff had disappeared with his men. He glanced wistfully at the mare.

If he could only use her speed, he would soon be at the heels of the men of the law. As it was, all her strength was useless to him, and all he could do was to swing down that trail at an Indian's dog trot.

The mare followed him, as usual, happily. But for once, he would almost rather have been alone. For he felt that he was running toward his doom and that he was hurrying like water down a gorge toward the plunge of a waterfall.

11

The sign of the six horses, which Barney followed, led straight away through the mountains and soon left the faint trail to blaze a more direct path. A mighty respect arose in Barney for both the sheriff and his men, and that respect grew as he saw the manner in which they slid their horses down great slopes and toiled up the almost perpendicular sides of ravines. But over such terrain, a man like Barney Dwyer could more than keep pace with them on foot.

In four hours he had sight of them; a wisp of dust was blowing on a mountain shoulder two miles away, and through the dust he saw the small forms of the riders.

After that he went on more carefully through the day, afraid to get too close, afraid to stay far off lest he should lose all sign of the party when it turned down some naked, rocky ravine. And all this while the red mare followed him like a mountain goat over rough and smooth.

The sheriff's party halted for lunch. Barney Dwyer, from the top of a great slope looked down through the trees and saw the party halted at the side of a glacial lake as blue as a bit of ocean. He saw their fire smoke, and hunger stabbed him through the midst of his body. He drew still nearer. Others had apparently camped there, and in a big tin boiler that had been blackened by many fires, the posse was cooking a stew, perhaps. Whatever they had managed to shoot on the way, rabbits or squirrels, would be cut up and mixed with chopped bacon, flavored with roots and herbs—if any of the party knew enough Indian lore to select the correct plants—and thickened with bits of hardtack or eaten with pone. Starvation searched Barney with many pains when he saw the party being served from that old boiler!

Afterward, the group lolled about to complete an hour's rest for man and horse, but finally they moved on into the woods opposite, and Barney came down like a ravening wolf on the camp. He had no hope, but when he looked into the boiler, he found that the sheriff's party had actually left at least two quarts of a most delicious mulligan at the bottom of the boiler. That he ate with more relish than anything he ever had tasted, and then, abandoning all precautions, he lay flat on his back beside the lake and slept for fifteen minutes.

When he stood up, he was a man remade. The absorbing hunger was pacified. He drank a final time from the lake, sparingly, and continued with the labor of following their trail all through the afternoon until darkness came, until, finally he had to keep close up and be guided more by the noise the posse made than by the starlight glimpses he could catch of them.

A slender sickle of a moon rose in the east through a clear sky, and by that light, as he issued from the forest onto a bald, level, upland plateau, he now saw the procession winding before him. It seemed that the group intended to journey all through the night, though the slowness of their movements proved that their horses were utterly beaten. They dipped out of view over the edge of a ravine. Barney, coming to the edge of the rock, saw them descending far beneath him down the jags of a trail that hugged the precipitous face of the cliff. Below them ran a straight, narrow flume of water, sweeping fast, but through a channel so smooth that hardly a sound of rushing came up to the keen ear of Barney.

At the bottom of the trail, the cliff gave back and afforded room between its foot and the edge of the water for a beach covered with shrubs and with big stones. There the posse halted, at last. There a fire was kindled, and the sight of it made Barney suddenly aware that the air of that mountain night was very cold.

The red mare, at this moment, snorted and ran to him. Something had startled her. Now he saw the nature of the alarm, for close behind him came half a dozen riders whose approach had been muffled to silence by the noise of the wind. They were spread out in a line that permitted no escape to Barney.

One man rode a little from the rest, demanding calmly: "Who's there?"

"My name is Barney Dwyer!" he answered. "And I am—"

"Dwyer!" suddenly exclaimed the familiar deep ringing voice of McGregor. "It's Barney Dwyer, for a fact. Close in on him, boys. Dwyer, don't budge."

And the quick, frightened voice of Sue Jones added in haste: "Don't harm him. I've told you what he is! Don't hurt him, Mack!"

They stood about Barney with their guns, and the moonlight slanted into savage faces.

McGregor stood among the rest. By his mere vague silhouette Barney could recognize him. He was saying: "Maybe you're right, Sue. I'll do him no harm if he's as simple as you say. Look here, Dwyer, what's the game you're up to now?"

"It was account of me," said Barney, "that poor Peary was caught by the sheriff. And so I'm following along. I'm hoping for a chance to get him free again."

"One to four—you'd try that, would you?" muttered McGregor. "You've been riding all day after 'em?"

"I've been walking. Didn't I tell you before that I can't ride the mare?"

"Wait a moment," said McGregor. He leaned and felt the inside of Barney's trousers from the calf of the leg to the heel. There was not a trace of perspiration from the horse. McGregor, straightening again, exclaimed: "Sue, you're right! The poor devil keeps the horse with him for a mascot, or something—not to use! He *is* a half-wit, and I've been a fool about him. Dwyer, you really mean that you'd try to tackle the four of 'em? How?"

He asked it with a mild derision, pointing down toward the dim forms that, at the bottom of the cliff, were moving about the fire.

"One man," said McGregor, "can hold the narrowness of that trail. How would you get at Peary, for instance, through those four men tonight?"

Barney answered instantly, for the thought had come to him at the very first, making him shiver: "I'd try to get down to that run of water, above the camp, and then float with it down to the fire. They wouldn't likely expect anyone to come in water as fast as that. I'd lie at the edge of the camp and wait for chances to help Peary. That's all."

"Yeah," drawled McGregor, stepping back. "He's only got a piece of a mind, not a whole one. But let me see you start the job, Dwyer. Boys, the rest of you scatter ahead. Ride straight on. You know where to cut through to the pass toward Coffeeville. We'll lie for the sheriff there and give him hell, and get Peary away. Hurry on. I'll stay here a minute to see what poor Dwyer is going to try!"

Barney was already working down the dangerous face of the rock, studying the narrow ledges that extended beneath him. He heard Susan Jones calling eagerly above him: "Come back, Barney! Please come back! This is only a way to kill yourself, not to do anything for Len Peary!"

He answered briefly: "What does it matter? The life of a half-wit isn't worth anything. There's no man or woman or child in the world that would miss me. There's only the mare, poor thing!"

For he could see the head of the red mare as she ventured to the very verge of the cliff to look down after her master. Something choked in the throat of Barney as he saw her; then down he went again. He heard the girl cry out, pursuing him with anxious words.

"*I* care about you, Barney. I know you're honest and kind. You can't help the harm that you've done! Come back while you still can."

But he climbed down rapidly, hurrying his descent for fear that voice should overmaster his courage and charm him to a standstill, and then draw him back to that world where he was no more than a chopping block for the scorn of every jester.

The wind, its strength gathed like liquid in a funnel, struck at him. He lost one handhold and swung like a pendulum over a drop of a hundred feet, but, recovering his grip, he went on with the descent.

Below him, the river shot by with a whisper. He clung to a rock on the verge of it, now, and saw it hurling past. In spite of its speed, in places it was so smooth that the shattered images of the stars appeared again, a riffle of foam whipped down the stream to mark the rate of its progress.

He tried it with his hands. It was snow water, fresh from the summits and of a power to spread numbness with electric speed through the body. But it seemed to Barney, as he leaned over the cold rush of the creek, that this was an easy way for a poor half-wit to pass out of this life into whatever nebulous region of bewilderment and sorrow is reserved for the souls of those who are not quick of mind.

So he lowered himself into the stream and was flung like a dry stick down the current. With hands stretched before him, he warded off a dozen times the dangers from sharp, reaching points of stone. Then he saw the yellow gleam of firelight, the black shadows of stone and of human forms. So he caught one of those projecting points that threatened him. His grip held. His body streamed out with the force of the water for an instant, and then he drew himself, shuddering, out on the beach.

In a narrow path of firelight that streamed between two of the boulders, he saw a man walk past him. He dared look no higher than the knees. He saw the gleam of the spoon-handled spurs, brightly gilded. And at the edge of the water that figure passed, looking down, gun in hand, no doubt, at the outstretched body of Barney.

No, the fellow merely stooped, filled a canteen with water and returned toward the fire.

Barney, breathing again, took heed of his surroundings. It was the deep, black shadow of a large rock that had blanketed him away from the unsuspecting gaze of that water carrier. In

that same shadow he could rise to his knees and peek from
side to side and over the top securely.

To his left was Len Peary, seated against a narrow projec-
tion of rock. In his hands, which were free, was a tin of
coffee, which he sipped comfortably while smoking a cigarette. They had secured him, simply, by passing the length of
a lariat around and around his body, then knotting it behind
the rock.

Two men had lain down, wrapped in their blankets, their
faces turned from the fire toward the cliff. Another sat on a
boulder with his back to the fire, a rifle across his knees,
while he kept watch on the trail that came down the face of
the cliff, the one apparent direction from which danger could
come at the party. The fourth man, now tending the coffee pot
at the fire, was the sheriff himself. He was humming a tune
contentedly, the short-stemmed pipe working up and down
between his teeth, now and then.

Barney worked snakelike to the rear of Peary's stone and
rapidly unfastened the knot that held the rope. Off to his left
the wall of the ravine was no longer a sheer face of rock, but
a steep slant of boulders of all sizes. Once he had Peary free,
perhaps they could dodge away to safety among those stones
and so climb up to the top of the bank. The shudder of cold
that was in the body of Barney Dwyer was not in his mind.
Whatever happened, his life was not a thing of importance.
He would never find, he was sure, a soul more tender and
sympathetic than that of the girl; and to her he was a mere
object of pitying contempt.

A sudden start that tugged on the coils of the rope, as the
knot came free in his fingers, told him that Len Peary was
aware of what was happening. He had to whisper: "Steady—
and watch your chances!"

He could see the sombrero of Len Peary nod in understanding above the top of the rock.

But now the sheriff came straight from the fire and sat
down cross-legged beside his prisoner.

"I can tell you this, Peary," he said, gravely. "If you make
a confession you'll probably get your life. And life in a
prison is better than a broken neck and the long night."

"I know," said Peary. "But the fact is that I didn't kill Buddy Marsh."

"You weren't even at the holdup, I suppose?" sneered the sheriff.

"I'm saying nothing about that," answered Peary. "But I'm telling you that I didn't kill Marsh. I've never pulled a trigger in my life until the other fellow was going for his gun."

"Do you stick on that?"

"I stick on that, because it's true," said Peary.

"Well," said the sheriff, "whatever the truth is, they have enough to hang you. And they'll do it. I don't pity you. It's what you have coming to you—you and all your kind. But because you're young, I was trying to show you the easiest way out."

"Thanks," said Peary. "But I still keep hoping."

"What sort of hope have you got?" asked Sheriff Elder. "The only thing that could get at us here would be a bird. And tomorrow we only have a few miles to get you into Coffeeville. Where's your hope, Peary?"

"I was born hoping; I'll keep on hoping till I die," said Peary carelessly.

And that was the moment that Barney chose. He rose from hands and knees. The sheriff, as though a shadow of peril whipped across his quick mind, jerked his head around over one shoulder, but Barney already had him by the arms, and so jerked him to his feet, and held him helpless.

Len Peary was up, also, shaking off the limp coils of the rope, and into the shout of the sheriff went the Indian yell of Peary as he snatched the revolver from the sheriff's holster.

The sentinel at the foot of the trail had leaped and whirled toward the noise. The pair who were wrapped in blankets rolled out again, reaching for their guns, but they saw their targets retreating, with the sheriff held as a protection before them. Back among the boulders they went, while Sheriff Jim Elder, maddened with shame and disappointment, cried out to his men to fire, regardless of his safety.

But they would not shoot through him to get at the other pair. All was confusion. One yelled one bit of advice, and one another, until, when they were high up the boulder-strewn slope, big Barney Dwyer released the sheriff.

The man ran down the way toward the frantic confusion of the forms around the fire, shouting orders as he went. But Dwyer and Leonard Peary were already on the level of the upper trail. The grip of Peary bit into the arm of Barney Dwyer.

"Some day, old timer—" said Peary. "Some day—"

He could not finish the remark. There was no need of finishing it. The tremor of his voice was enough.

Big Mack and the girl were on them, and the red mare came to Barney, sniffing him curiously, snorting, and then pawing at the ground.

"We saw that by the firelight," said McGregor. "We saw the shadow of you all the time, and of all the cool bits of devilry that I ever saw—well, you're alive, Peary, and that's more than you have a right to be!"

"He ought not to have turned the sheriff loose!" complained Len Peary. "We all could have said a few things to that fellow Elder. What's the matter, Sue? What are you crying about? Let's get out of here!"

"I'm crying because I've found out what a hero is," said the girl.

"They're coming pretty fast!" exclaimed McGregor. "They're coming on the trail fast, and they're well-mounted, the lot of 'em. Len, pop into the saddle on the pinto!"

"It's Sue's horse!" said Peary.

"I'm talking about the saving of your neck, man," cried McGregor. "They won't hurt a woman—or a dunce that happens to be a hero! Len, jump on that horse and come with me!"

And Peary, to the bewilderment of Barney, actually sprang on the pinto and galloped away with McGregor!

12

They had reason for their going that beat louder and louder in their ears as the posse drove its horses as hard as possible up the steep slope of the cliff trail. The sheriff had straightened out all the confusion of his men and now he brought them on with a savage rush.

From his horse, Peary had cried out: "Scatter, Sue and Barney. They won't bother you. They'll tackle us! Scatter and lie low!"

"They've left us—they've left *you*, Barney. I won't believe it! Try the mare—try the mare and ride for your life, if you can! Oh, Barney—the traitors!"

As for Barney, he moved in a dream, dimly. They might have shared the horses. They might have stayed to fight. Perhaps they would have done this, except that McGregor realized that his was the only rifle in his party; and revolvers are poor things for moonlight shooting.

But they had fled with hardly a word!

He went to the mare and fitted his foot into the stirrup, not because he had hope, but because his back was so against the wall. Then he swung into the saddle and sat loosely, waiting for the explosion that would hurl him into the air.

Instead, the mare merely lifted her head and turned it, looking back at him with ears pricked. There was not a tremor in her powerful body. She was still as a stone!

In the meantime, the posse was near. Their voices seemed already to have topped the rimrock and to be rushing at the fugitives. Far away, the forms of McGregor and Len Peary were dwindling in the moonlight; but Barney Dwyer would be in the very jaws of danger.

He reined the mare across the neck. At the first touch of pressure she turned readily, and the heart of Barney leaped. She was his, and it was not strength that had conquered her. Even in the terror of that moment, and the haste, he had time to realize that there *is* a force of beauty and mystery of life far different from the brutal ways of most men.

He stretched his hand to the girl.

"She's tamed, Sue!" he called to her. "And she's strong enough to carry us both. Get up behind me—"

She waved him frantically away with both hands.

"Go on!" she shouted. "They won't hurt me. I'm only a woman. Save yourself, Barney! Don't—"

"I'll stay here, then," said Barney simply.

When she saw him so calmly immovable, she put her foot on the stirrup, and was instantly up behind him. And as Barney patted the shoulder of the red mare, she broke into a gallop as long, as free, as swift as though there were not a feather's weight upon her back!

Every stride was a long step toward safety, but the mare was hardly in motion before Elder and his men were on the upper plateau. They could hear his voice, shouting: "Mike! Pete! Take the girl and Dwyer, yonder. I'm going after Peary and the other. Ride like the devil and then come back on my trail."

So, while two riders swept off after McGregor and Peary, two more came like yelling Indians after Barney and the girl. When Barney looked back, it seemed to him that those flying mustangs must surely overtake him in an instant, but still the long stroke of the mare's gallop kept them at their distance. How she could have swept away from them with only a single burden on her back!

If she could last until they reached the dark cloud of trees that rolled up on the other side of the little plateau, then there might be a chance to dodge away to safety. Toward that goal, Barney directed her. Gallantly she ran, but almost instantly the immense strain began to tell. Her ears flattened; a shudder of effort came in every stride.

And the girl cried close to the ear of Barney Dwyer: "Let me drop off, Barney. Then you'll be off like a bird. Let me drop here, or I'll throw myself to the ground—they won't bother about me. They'll go on after you, and—"

Her right arm was firmly about him. He caught that arm and held it in a vise. "When you have to stop, I have to stop with you," he said quietly. "We've still got a ghost of a chance!"

He heard her groan with despair; but the grip of her arm tightened around him. Joy came over him like a light, like a madness. To her, he might be no more than a dolt, a half-wit, but for this moment they were sweeping on to a single destiny.

Behind them he heard the pounding of hoofs that seemed to

make the earth beneath them tremble. But here were the woods, black caverns of shadow.

Under those shadows he swept. The beds of pine needles almost silenced the noise of hoofs; yet the pair were so close behind that he could feel the beating of the hoofs.

He crashed the mare through a tangle of shrubbery, dodged into a region of vast shadow under the pine trees, and suddenly halted the mare beside a great trunk. Both of them slid to the ground and waited. Straight toward them came the noise of the pursuers, the pounding hoofs, the creaking of the stirrup leathers. Two dim shapes drew into view, pressed nearer, and went by! They passed through a little silver streak of moonlight, and were gone.

So the two stood in a silence. Barney heard the labored breathing of the mare. With every inhalation the cinch straps creaked a little.

"We'd better go on," said Barney. "They might stop going ahead and begin to hunt for us on the back trail."

He walked slowly on, at right angles to the direction in which they had fled. The girl hurried to get into step with him. She was on one side. On the other, his hand rested affectionately on the mane of the red mare. And so they went by the big trees, quietly, never speaking, until they came to a point where the trees left off for a moment, and the shoulder of the mountain dropped swiftly away before them. Through the moon haze they looked far off at mountain shapes, only real and clear where the light glistened on the upper reaches of snow and of ice. Out of the black of the canyon below them a voice of water kept booming softly, like the beating of great kettle drums and the blowing of distant horns.

Sue stretched an arm out, pointing.

"You're like that, Barney," she said. "There's more scope to you than to millions of the men I've known. If ever I've hurt you—"

"I'm used to pain," said Barney, earnestly. "It doesn't matter. And I'm so happy now that I want to shout. Only, shouting wouldn't say it at all."

Part
Two

13

Beyond the pine trees, the trail dipped through a green hollow, and McGregor and Peary took this better going at the full gallop, letting their horses stretch out to the work. Peary leaned forward to jockey his horse ahead, with the enthusiasm of a boy riding a race for fun or a wager. McGregor, sitting straight in the saddle, seemed to let his horse run of its own unguided will, yet he kept even with his companion; and looking at the iron of his face, it was easier to realize that murder was the goal he aimed at.

Before them, in the midst of the hollow, they saw an old man jogging along on a mule. The hump of his shoulders and the outstanding ridge of his backbone showed his years, and as Peary shot past he had a glimpse of a long white face, and under the brows, dark eyes like a death's-head. This ancient man waved a greeting to McGregor. His hand was a skeleton's claw.

The two passed on up the farther slope, left the trail, climbed a hill, and drew rein behind a clump of trees through whose trunks they could see the white of a road just beneath.

"Here we are," said McGregor. "Barney Dwyer and the girl ought to be coming along this way before long."

"But look there!" exclaimed Peary. "That old idiot on the mule is coming after us. He'll spoil everything!"

"He won't spoil anything," answered McGregor. "That old idiot is Doc Adler!"

"Who is he?" asked Peary.

McGregor turned on Peary a dull eye, as one who is not sure that an explanation will be worthwhile. Then he said briefly: "Doc Adler has killed more men than smallpox and made more money than the mint. Now he's retired to private life as a sort of universal uncle to crooks who know enough to ask his advice. And we need it now!"

Adler rode his mule over the brow of the hill, at that moment, and came straight on.

"Now, boys! Now, boys!" he said, as he came up. "What's in the air?"

"A pretty girl and a half-wit," said McGregor. "They ought to be coming up this road, in a few minutes. This fellow is Len Peary, Doc. He wants the girl; and I want the man—dead!"

"Well," said Doc Adler, "maybe I'm gettin' old and feeble in the brain, but how could a poor fool bother a pair like you two?"

"Because there's no fear in him," said McGregor, frowning. "He took Peary away from under my nose, so to speak. And everybody in the mountains knows, now, that Barney Dwyer made a fool of me. That's why he has to die, Doc. If I lose my reputation, where am I?"

"Nowhere," agreed Adler. He fixed the dark hollows of his eyes on McGregor and nodded to confirm his judgment. Then he patted the butt of the Winchester that lay in its long saddle scabbard under his left knee. "This here might speak a word that would put an end to Barney Dwyer, Mack! What keeps you from taggin' him out with a slug of lead?"

"Because the girl's with him," answered McGregor. "And Peary wants her more than he wants eyes in his head. If we drop Dwyer out of her hand, so to speak, she won't have to guess about who turned the trick. She's another one with clean hands, Doc. It turned her sick to think of Peary on the road with me; and one killing would finish him, as far as she's concerned."

"Birds of a feather oughta flock together," said old Doc Adler to Peary. "You look a bright, upstandin' kid. You oughta know she ain't your breed. It'd be an outcross. Leave her be, boy! Leave her alone. Tag Dwyer with a chunk of lead and let him lie."

Peary looked at the old villain in silence.

"It's no good, Doc," said McGregor. "I'll take care of Barney Dwyer as soon as I get him away from the girl. But I can't take him by force—not if there's any other way!"

"They're coming!" broke in Peary, pointing through a gap in the trees.

"Get the horses and the mule back from the head of the hill," ordered McGregor, dismounting. "Get off the mule, Doc, and lend me your brains."

Doc Adler got down to the ground with remarkable agility, and as Peary obediently took the livestock out of view, Adler was smiling. Into the shadows of his eyes came a light.

"Gimme that field glass of yours, McGregor," said he. It was handed over to him, and as he busily focused it through the trees on the advancing pair, he muttered: "The back of the legs, that's where a man gets old first, and then in the small of the back, and then in the shoulders, and then in the eyes, and then in the brain. I'm old clean up to my eyes, Mack, but there's a part of the brain left yet, I guess!"

He steadied the glass and then murmured: "The man's walkin' and the girl's ridin'. But the way she keeps dippin' and bendin' toward him, you'd think that she'd rather be walking on the ground with him than settin' dead comfortable in that saddle."

"I'm glad that Peary isn't seeing it, then," answered McGregor.

"This here boy, this here Peary," said old Doc Adler, "is he the right sort to be useful to you?"

"He's all right, but he hasn't made up his mind, yet," said McGregor. "He wants a free life. He hates work. He hates his father's ranch. He can fight like a tiger. And he's fast with

a gun, and straight. But being outside the law is a game with
him, so far. It's fun for him, and not a business. He doesn't
mind stealing, but he hates stolen money. He'd rather take the
money one day and give it back the next. But I think I've got
my hands on him, now. He loaned a hand in a stage robbery,
not long ago, and I fixed it so that the shooting of the driver
is laid to him. I did that shooting myself, but so long as the
sheriff thinks that Peary turned the trick, it's enough to hang
him. Fear of the rope will make Peary what I want him to be,
in the long run.''

"You're a bright boy, Mack," said Doc Adler. "You got
brains. When I was young, I would of wanted a partner, like
you." He broke off to say, "That's considerable of a hoss that
the girl is riding."

"It's a wild-caught mustang," said McGregor. "Dwyer
tamed her, and nobody but Dwyer could ride her, up to a little
while ago. But now I see he's let the girl make friends with
the mare."

"A wild-caught mustang is like a wild-caught hawk," said
Doc Adler. "They fly the best. There's something in that girl,
too. She carries her head like there was something inside of
it; and she's got a pretty face."

"She's as clean as a dog's tooth, and very nearly as
sharp," said McGregor. "But get that brain of yours working, Doc, will you? How am I to stop that pair from riding
straight on into Coffeeville? I mean, without using guns. If
the girl gets away, Peary will tag along after her, all over the
world. And if Dwyer gets away from me, everybody in
the mountains will be laughing at me!''

Doc Adler lowered the glasses. He turned to McGregor and
rested his hand against the rough bark of a pine tree.

"If I stopped 'em, and parted 'em, and sent the man away
from the girl, what would I get out of it?" asked Adler.

"Stop them—part them—send the man away—how the
devil can you do that, Doc?" asked McGregor.

"By brainwork, son," said Doc Adler. "You can go up
ahead, you and Peary, and pretty soon, I'll send Dwyer
galloping along on that red mare. You can shoot him off of

that hoss and the girl will know nothing except that he never came back to her. But what would I get out of it?''

"What would you want, Doc?" asked McGregor.

"The mare!" said Adler, suddenly, eagerly.

"The mare?" echoed McGregor. "But what would you do with her? You couldn't ride her!"

"Does a charm on a watch chain help a watch to keep time?" asked Adler, snarling. "No, and I want the mare not to ride, but just to have. Understand?"

"I don't understand, but she's yours," said McGregor. "How the devil you can manage these things, I don't know. But I'm going to take your word. I'll ride up the road and wait there with Peary. And if you send Barney Dwyer past us alone, and on the mare, I'll call you a wizard, Adler!"

14

The road was more bumps than level, more rocks than soil, but Barney Dwyer stepped over it with his head high and his eyes fixed on the mountains at which he could look through the double fence of the high, dark pine trees. As the road changed, swerved, twisted snakelike back and forth as mountain trails will do, he had an everchanging viewpoint and an everchanging view. But what he saw of them, blue or brown or shining white, was not what filled his soul and kept him smiling; it was the girl, who rode on the red mare beside him, tilting toward Barney, laughing and chatting.

"Even the mare knows you, Sue," said Barney. "And even the mare loves you!"

"As long as you're with me," said the girl. "But if you were away, she'd pitch me into the air and step on me when I hit the ground."

"She'd never buck with you, Sue," said Dwyer.

"I can see the side-flare in her eyes, and her ears are

trembling, and she keeps stretching the reins to make sure that her head belongs to herself," said the girl.

"Jog her ahead," said Barney Dwyer. "You'll see that she's as gentle as a lamb, with you."

"She'll turn me into a skyrocket," said Sue Jones. "But I don't mind trying her."

She slapped the shoulder of the red mare, which started instantly off at a long, gliding trot, with head turned to the side as a horse will turn it in order to look back at the home place when a journey begins. But when the mare came to the next bend of the road, rather than round it and pass out of the master's sight, she suddenly bounded into the air and landed on stiff legs and with arched back. The shock almost slung the girl from the saddle, but with knee and hand she clung to it; and before the red mare leaped again, the shout of Barney Dwyer checked her like a rope. He ran up as the girl straightened herself, gasping, pulled her sombrero level, and looked down at Barney.

"She's a pretty dry stick of dynamite, Barney," she said. "But I told you so!"

Barney Dwyer shook his head. He walked on beside the mare, smoothing the silk of her neck with his hand, speaking to her reproachfully.

"You can't blame her," commented Sue Jones. "She was never broke; she was just gentled. You can't make her fear you, but you can make her love you!"

They rounded that curve that the mare had refused to pass the moment before, and they saw before them a figure huddled facedown at the edge of the road. His arms were stretched out before him, and an old black hat lay under one limp hand. The long, silver hair blew like a mist in the wind.

The girl uttered a cry; Barney ran forward and leaned by the fallen body.

It was warm. He made sure of that with the first touch of his hand. Gently he turned the old man until he could see a long, deathly white face. The closed eyes seemed to be painted over with black.

He pressed his ear to the breast and, after a moment, he made out the beating of the heart.

So Barney straightened up on his knees and shouted to the girl: "He's living!"

"I saw his breast move," she said.

She was very calm, leaning above the fallen man.

"He's pegged out on the road," said Barney, making his voice soft, as though for fear that limp body might hear him. "Think of it, Sue! An old man like this—and thrown out to die, like—well, the way some people let old horses loose to starve on the road!"

"That's the way the world is," said the girl. "He has a queer look about him. He's either a saint or a devil, I'd say."

"He's a dying man," said Barney. "Nothing but a doctor or a priest can help him! Let's get him off the road, and into some sort of comfort!"

He picked up that loose, sagging body, and carried it into the shadow of the nearest pine tree. The girl was already there, kicking together, and then smoothing down, a bed of pine needles. On that, Barney Dwyer laid the helpless form.

And almost at once the old man opened his eyes.

He said: "It's all right, Harry. I'm wore out. You go on. I'll never be no good no more. You go on!"

Then, from under frowning brows, he centered his gaze on Barney Dwyer, and was silent.

"Who is Harry?" asked Dwyer.

"It don't matter," said the old fellow.

"It was Harry that left you lying on the ground?" asked the girl suddenly.

It rather shocked Barney Dwyer to see that she stood back from the victim, frowning a little as she looked down at him. She had not expressed the slightest concern from the beginning.

"Harry had to go on. I needed to rest a mite," said the old man. "I just sat down and took a rest—that was all."

"You fell on your face!" exclaimed Barney Dwyer. "You walked till you dropped! What's your name? No, don't answer that! I'll get you some water!"

He took a canteen from the saddle of the mare, and ran to the nearest sound of flowing water. The mare trotted after him like a dog; and the old man on the bed of pine needles closed his eyes.

"Will you tell me your name?" asked the girl, standing close by and tilting her head to one side, very much like a magpie studying a new sight.

"It's all right, Harry," muttered the other. "You go on first—and I'll come slow along. You go on—"

His voice died away.

"What day is it?" asked the girl, sharply.

He opened his eyes and stared feebly, helplessly toward her.

"Monday, ma'am," said he.

"Humph!" murmured Sue Jones. "It's Tuesday. You've been lying out there in the road for twenty-four hours?"

"I don't know," said the other. "I just seem to remember walkin' along, and then—I don't remember nothin' else!"

Barney Dwyer came back on the run with the canteen. He raised the head of the old man gently, and tilted the canteen to his lips. The old fellow took only a swallow and then relaxed to limpness, sliding from the hand of Dwyer until he was flat on the bed of pine needles again.

"Barney!" said the girl.

He came hesitantly toward her, his head still turned back to look at the sufferer.

"Barney," she went on, very quietly at his ear. "This may all be a fake. Every bit of it! He talks as though he'd lain in the road for a day. But last night there was a rain. There are no dust and rain spots, as there ought to be, if he'd lived through all of that weather! There's nothing about his clothes to show that he's been out in the weather."

"Why, he was under the trees when it rained, I suppose," said Barney Dwyer. "What d'you men, Sue?"

"I mean," she answered, "that he may not be honest."

"Not honest? Not honest?" said Barney. "Sue, what can be in your mind? Why—see how white his face is!"

"Age does that, sometimes," she replied coldly.

"But he's all thin and worn!" said Barney.

"Age will do that, too!"

"He was fainting, when we saw him!" said Barney.

"Maybe that's a sham, too," she decided. "You have to

remember that McGregor is somewhere in the field against you, Barney. And Peary is against you, too.''

"Why should Peary be against me?" asked Dwyer, staring.
"Perhaps he'd be in jail except for me, Sue."

"I'm the reason," said the girl, flushing. "You know, Barney, that a girl understands when a man really wants her. And Len Peary wanted me."

"Did you want him?" asked Barney, naively.

"I didn't know you, then," she answered. "Yes, I would have married him, I think. Except that I knew he was friends with McGregor. That held me back."

Dwyer looked long at her.

"Anybody who once hoped to have you would do murders to keep you," he declared. "But how could McGregor or Peary have anything to do with this?"

"I don't know," she answered. "But I know that they're you're enemies, and that makes me suspect everything that happens to us until we're out of this part of the country."

Barney took off his hat and began to pass his fingers through his hair.

"We've got to do something about the poor old man!" said Barney Dwyer. "Suspicion won't put him on his feet!"

"Maybe he's well enough to get up and walk—if he has to. Maybe he's strong enough to run, as a matter of fact!" she replied.

"You feel that way, and I'm sorry," said Barney. "But you know better than I do. What shall we do, then?"

She looked around her furtively toward the trees, as though she half expected danger to leap out from behind them at any moment.

"The thing for us to do," she finally said, "is for me to stay here with him, while you ride on into Coffeeville. It won't take you long. In an hour or so you can be back from the town with a doctor in a buckboard. And then, if this old wreck is honest, we can take him away where he'll be properly cared for."

"But leaving you behind?" he asked. "No, I see the point. If you come with me, the poor old man is helpless and alone.

Stay here, Sue, and I'll be back as fast as the red mare can fetch and carry me.''

He jumped into the saddle on the mare and galloped her out of sight, out of hearing before the girl, at last, turned back toward her patient and found him sitting up on his bed of pine needles, looking at her with the eyes of a death's-head.

15

For a half mile the long, elastic stride of the red mare carried Barney up the road toward Coffeeville, twinkling through the tree shadows and the alternate strips of sunshine. There was a darkness in his mind, because he could not understand what had seemed to him cruelly cold suspicion in the attitude of Sue Jones to the old man they had found. So his thoughts were far ahead of him and his eyes were seeing nothing. For that matter, he did not need to keep a lookout, and he knew it. His senses never could be so alert as those of the mare that bore him.

She, with her head high and her ears pricked, studied every breath of wind with suspicious nostrils, and examined every sparkle of the sun on a leaf, every stir and shifting far back among the shadows of the woods.

Now what she suddenly saw as she cantered around a bend of the road was no more than another glint of light very similar to the flash of the sun on a bit of varnished green foliage. Very similar, but slightly different. This luminous streak had a harder brilliance, and the mare halted with such a sudden shock that Barney was flung forward across her neck.

Through the space he would have filled if he had been still erect whined two rifle bullets. One was as high as his heart, and one was as high as his head.

The mare did what she would have done on the open range, if a mountain lion had leaped up beside her path. She waited for no orders but bolted through a clump of poplars and took Barney out on the other side into the midst of bigger trees.

Four more bullets had rattled through the greenery as they fled. Then Barney heard the beat of hoofs; he heard the familiar voice of McGregor, ringing like an iron horn, as it cried, "Drive straight through, Peary! We've got to get him! We've got to get him!"

Barney had neither rifle nor revolver, but he had the mare. She took him through the dark of the forest like a jagged streak of red lightning.

When she came out on the farther side of the woods, instead of running straight on, she turned to the right and skimmed along under the edges of the trees, aiming toward a little ridge of ground beyond which they would be shut from view."

Barney, totally bewildered, merely clung to the horn of the saddle with one hand, and with the other grasped the loosely hanging reins. The mare not only ran but did his thinking for him.

Looking back, Barney saw the two riders dash out from the trees into the open. He saw the flash of their long rifles. They reined in their mounts for an instant, looking for the prey. At last they saw it, but only as the mare dipped over the rising ground like a red streak and sank into the hollow beyond as a swallow swings down that open green valley between the hills through the air.

Still she was fending for herself, and this was not to her liking. She knew all about rifles. In those old days when she ran free across the range, many a foolish cowpuncher that had failed to run her down had tried to capture her by "creasing." Twice her neck had been slashed by bullets.

So she knew that there was no space for her to get out of range before the two riders behind had topped the hill. So while that barrier still rose behind her, she slanted back into the strip of woods again, and darting through it to the road, her powerful stride snatched Barney around the curves and over high and low toward Coffeeville. He heard behind him the rattling of hoofs on rocks, the pounding of them on softer ground. Once Peary and McGregor had a glimpse of him as he rounded a long curve, and they both fired again. But he did not even hear the slinging of the bullets, and after that there was pleasant silence down the road behind him.

They were gone, and before him was Coffeeville, scattered along one side of Green Creek in the midst of green pasture lands. On the other side of the creek stood the pine forest.

Barney called the mare back to a dog trot. He had dropped the guns of McGregor and Peary out of striking distance behind him, but the town itself might hold danger enough for him. If Sheriff Elder or any of his posse were there, they would be sure to recognize him; and since he had taken Peary away from them all, they would be as anxious to get at him as greyhounds are to put their teeth in a fleeing rabbit. Barney and the girl had talked over the danger of this chance, but they had determined to risk it. For the railroad tapped Coffeeville with the farthest extension of its line, and they wanted the speed of trains to sweep them away from McGregor's pursuit.

So Barney jogged slowly into Coffeeville, praying with all his heart that the sheriff with his men might be out combing the woods, searching through the mountains. A bare-legged boy came out from a house lugging over his shoulder a heavy, long-barreled rifle as old as the old frontier.

"Can you tell me if there's a doctor in this town?" asked Barney politely.

"*You* got a hoss!" said the boy. "What a whale *that* hoss is! I reckon she can move, mister, eh?"

"She's fast," agreed Barney. "Is there a doctor in the town?"

"She's got a neck like a stallion on her, ain't she?" said the boy. "Yeah. Down there at the other end of town you'll see a white house with a green roof onto it. That's where Dr. Swain hangs out, mostly. Hey, are you Barney Dwyer?"

Barney did not answer.

Far down the street, rounding a curve, he glanced back and saw that the boy was coming, rifle and all, at a scamper.

But here was the end of the town, and a white house with a veranda built across the face of it, and a green roof above. It was just the sort of a place one would expect a doctor to live in. There was an air of neatness and order such as a professional man would demand of his surroundings.

Barney dismounted and left the mare at the hitching rack, where a saddled horse already was standing, a great rough-made brute of a brown gelding.

Barney passed through the front gate and left it swinging behind him, the iron latch clanking softly as it flicked across the catch. The front steps were painted blue. So was the floor of the veranda. And Barney stood in awe at the door, hat in hand, smoothing his hair a little before he knocked.

In answer to his tap, there loomed down the hallway an immense man, a fitting burden for the huge horse in the street.

"Well?" he asked, in a heavy voice. "Well, young man?"

"I beg your pardon," said Barney, "I only wanted to ask—"

"Nothing here for beggars. Not even a woodpile. Get along with you," said the giant.

"I only wanted to ask—" said Barney, retreating half a step.

"Get off this place!" roared the big man in a sudden fury. "And get off quick, or I'll throw you off. Away with you, and all the rest of the worthless, lazy loafers in the mountains!"

He cast open the screen door, which crashed with a metallic jangling behind him, as he stood towering above Barney. And the blue, mild eyes of Barney rounded with awe.

"Are you Dr. Swain?" he asked.

"I'm Dr. Swain," said the giant. "And I'll doctor you, young man, if you don't get off—"

"I'm sorry," said Barney. "I don't want to trouble you, but I'm not exactly begging for anything—I want you to come to see a sick man yonder in the woods—"

"Not begging—sick man in the woods—what's he sick of?" exclaimed the doctor.

The small boy with the rifle had now arrived in a thin cloud of dust. He stood gripping the front fence and staring at the big pair on the veranda.

"I don't know what he's sick of," said Barney. "I just found him—"

"What's his name?"

"I don't know," said Barney gravely.

"D'you know anything at all?" shouted the doctor, his anger blasting its way out again.

"No, sir. I don't know very much," said Barney, sighing.

"I'm a busy man. I've got no time to talk to fools!" said the doctor. "Get off this place and stay off!"

"D'you mean that you won't come!" exclaimed Barney, incredulous.

For doctors were to him among the saints of the world. They were the stayers of pain, the open-handed friends of the poor. Therefore he could not believe the words that the doctor now roared at him: "I've told you ten times, to get out! Now I'll show you the way to the gate!"

With that, Dr. Swain laid on the arm of Barney a grasp that never yet had been successfully resisted. But now, under the iron type of his fingers, he felt the arm of Barney turn from soft to rubbery hard that twisted suddenly like a snake, out of the grip.

"If you won't come of your own free will, I'll have to take you," said Barney.

"Take me?" shouted the furious doctor. "Take me?"

He was so angry that he struck suddenly at the face of Barney, not with his fist, but with the back of his hand. There was weight enough in that mere gesture to have floored an ordinary man, but it glanced from Barney like a stinging raindrop. He caught Dr. Swain by both wrists and held him so. The doctor, with a grunt of astonishment, tried to wrench away. His effort merely turned the hold of Barney into bracelets of red-hot iron that shrank into the flesh and ground the tendons against the bones.

"Who are you?" asked the doctor.

It was the boy at the fence who answered, with a yell: "You can't get away from him, Doc Swain. He's Barney Dwyer! He's Barney Dwyer for sure!"

That name dissolved the last strength of resistance in Swain. It was the most amazing instant of Barney's life, and he had to say gently, "There'll be no danger and no harm to you, Dr. Swain, if you'll come along quietly."

"In the middle of broad daylight—right out of my house!" muttered the doctor.

But he shook his great head and went with Barney down the path toward the gate.

"I should have known by the mare," grumbled Swain, chafing his bruised wrists. "The Lord knows there's been enough talk about the red mare and Barney Dwyer. Young man," he broke out in a fervor, "if you had ten necks, there are nevertheless ten ropes that will hang all of 'em, one of these days!"

"I hope I didn't hurt you," said Barney, anxiously. "I didn't want to hurt you. But d'you mind hurrying a little? You see, people are running out in the street, and they may begin to shoot at me any moment!"

The doctor put his foot in the stirrup, but hesitated an instant to stare at Barney's mild face. Then he swung into the saddle with a grunt.

And down the street dodged the screeching voice of the boy with the rifle, crying: "Come look! He's here! Barney Dwyer's in town! Barney Dwyer!"

They were coming to look, too. Men and women and children rushed out of houses and shops, but the big gelding and the red mare were already at a gallop, swinging across the open range.

16

When Sue Jones, turning from the road, saw the old man sitting up, and felt the skull-like darkness of those eyes fixed on her, she gave back several hurried steps. There was nothing about his age that she could fear, she told herself, but a strange premonition and a sense of evil came over her, cold as the gliding of a snake.

He had sunk back again until his shoulders sagged against

the trunk of the pine tree. A squirrel ran down to a lower branch and sat up to scold at the intruder.

"Lie down," said Sue, hurrying back, and filled instantly with shame. "You mustn't sit up. Save your strength and lie down! Do you feel better now?"

"I was kind of tuckered out," said the man. "I jus' kind of give out, suddenlike. But I guess I'm all right now, once I could get onto my feet, again! Will you gimme a help, ma'am?"

"You must lie down. Do as I tell you," said the girl. "There'll be a doctor here in a few minutes. You'll be taken care of. Don't worry about that!"

"I'd like to stand up," said he. "Wouldn't you lend me a help, ma'am?"

"It will only show you how weak you are," said Sue, and held out her brown, strong young hand to assist him.

Over her wrist fastened the white claw of the other. She gasped with terror, but her effort to wrench away merely helped to pull him to his feet. She could shake him, but she could not burst away from him, and this she understood at once. On tiptoe, eyes dilated, for an instant she trembled with her terror. But the moment she knew that she was helpless, she stood quietly resigned. She took hold of her fear with the strength of her will and mastered it.

"That's better," said the old man. "That's a lot better. Jest calm and easy is the trick, my beauty."

She looked at the old devil as a man looks, eye to eye. Even her voice was perfectly steady when she said, "I suspected something. I felt the devil in you, from the first."

"I seen you did," said Doc Adler. "There was a coupla times when I was afraid that *you* would put a finger on my pulse. And I couldn't fool you then no more than I could fool a doctor. You're bright enough. Oh, you're plenty bright enough. And there's enough fire in you to cook many a man, I reckon. Yeah, bake him tender right to the wishbone. But if—"

Here they heard the distant explosions of guns, sounding very much like hammer strokes through the thinness of the mountain air. Six shots the girl counted, and at every one of them her body jerked a little, as though the bullets had struck home in her own flesh.

"Barney—" she whispered, staring at the hollow eyes of Adler.

He favored her with his toothless, evil grin.

"That's the end of him," said Adler. "I reckon that McGregor would finish him, all right. McGregor ain't the man to miss four times running!"

Curiously, Adler watched the bluish tinge come into her face. She began to breathe spasmodically.

And now, from a greater distance, two rifle shots again. It was Adler's time to start.

"They missed him the first time! They've missed him again. God wouldn't let him die!" cried the girl.

The life came back to her as she spoke.

Old Adler snarled: "Four bullets sunk in him, and the mare carries him a ways, and then he drops out of the saddle, after a while. And McGregor comes up and looks at him lyin' there on the ground, and writhin', and wrigglin'. Not dead, but dyin'. So he puts in two more shots, just to make sure. Two more shots, and that turns Barney Dwyer into a soggy lump of nothin'!"

His lips began to twitch over that gaping grin.

The girl shook her head.

"They missed the first four times, and then they missed again. The red mare would have him a lot farther away by that time. She'd carry him like a stone running downhill, faster and faster, if she ran for her life. He's safe, now. He's safe in Coffeeville. I know it!"

"If he is," said Adler, with bitter venom, "then there ain't any truth or rightness in McGregor and his guns. And I'll be done with him, and may the devil fly off with him!"

So they remained for a long moment, the hand of Adler frozen onto the wrist of the girl, until the rapid pounding of hoofs beat on their ears, and down the road came McGregor, galloping his horse hard; behind him, on a rope, labored the mule of Doc Adler.

He drew up, throwing the rope end toward Adler.

"Here's your mule, Doc," said he. "Climb aboard it. Sue, jump up here behind me!"

Adler released her wrist. She looked down for an instant at the white marks that surrounded her arm. Then she walked slowly toward McGregor.

"He got away, Mack," she declared.

"Who?" said McGregor, frowning.

"Barney Dwyer. You missed him. He's safe in Coffeeville!"

"He's safe in Coffeeville till the sheriff picks him up and the crowd strings him up to a tree," answered McGregor. "Jump up here behind me!"

"Tell me one thing, please!" she begged.

"Well, what is it?"

"Was Len Peary with you? Were you alone, or was Len Peary with you?"

"Peary?" answered McGregor, looking straight back into her eyes. "If he'd been with me, d'you think that he would have helped against Barney? He owes Dwyer his life, and he's too soft to forget that sort of a thing!"

She hesitated, and then nodded. "I think he's soft enough to know what gratitude is, Mack," she agreed. "Where are you going to take me?"

He smiled, but his eyes went savage as he stared down at her.

"You know how they catch wild hawks, Sue?" said he. "They tie a pigeon with a string, and when the hawk flies over, it swoops right down into a net. You'll be the pigeon for me, Sue. That fool of a lucky half-wit will never stop hunting till he finds you, and when he finds you, he'll find me and my guns. Climb up behind me. It's late—and we've a ways to go!"

She made no resistance, not even with a word. Talking and struggling would be folly, she knew.

"Go first, Doc," said McGregor. "You know the way to your own house."

"My own house?" shouted Adler, in a sudden passion. "Am I gonna show the whole world where I live?"

"Go on, Doc," said McGregor. "You're in this with me,

and you're going to stay in with me. I'll tell you the whole idea when we're alone. Start on!''

Adler looked at him out of those baleful eyes for a moment, but then, surrendering as quietly as the girl had done, he rode across the trail and went up the slope among the pine trees.

17

That is why Barney Dwyer, riding in among the trees, found empty the place where he had left the old man and the girl. He jumped down from his horse, stared at the untenanted bed of pine needles, and then wandered helplessly in a circle, like an animal tethered to a stake.

Dr. Swain said nothing. During the ride from Coffeeville, he had not talked a great deal, but he had been able to shake off the sense of fear that had possessed him when he left the town. Gradually he came to realize that he had met that impossible thing—a man who had no desire for physical supremacy, one who felt no glory in a triumph.

And the doctor's sense of wounded pride vanished. He asked questions. He received honest answers about the strange way in which Barney Dwyer had undertaken the quest for Leonard Peary; and it was at this point that the two men rode through the trees to the place where Dwyer found nothing but the heaped-up pine needles.

"They've gone," said Barney, helplessly. "I don't understand! She couldn't have carried him away."

A sudden suspicion made the doctor exclaim: "Well, could he have carried *her* away?"

"Why," said Barney, always willing to repeat everything patiently, "he was very old, you know, and so weak and sick that he could not move. I had to carry him. His poor head and arms and legs hung down. It was like carrying a dead body!"

"Wait a moment," said the doctor. "Tell me what he looks like. I've ridden every inch of this range to my patients, and I know a good many thousand faces."

"Well, he's old and white; and he has a white, long face; and his eyes are like the black holes in a skull—"

"Adler!" shouted the doctor. "Doc Adler!"

He lowered his voice. The violence with which he had shouted seemed to frighten him, suddenly. He listened, hushed, to the echoes as they fled away.

"Adler? Who is he?" asked Barney Dwyer.

"Adler is what nobody knows—except that he's a devil. Except that he's committed every crime on the calendar, no one knows what he's done. Everything from picking pockets to murder. But nothing ever has been proved against him. He has always known how to cover his trail. Adler? God pity that poor girl!"

"But it was an old, helpless, sick man!" cried Dwyer.

"An old man like that could pretend to be helpless and sick, Dwyer. Don't you realize that?"

Barney stretched out his hands as though to grasp something out of the empty air. He looked down at those hands, then struck them against his forehead.

"I'll try to find her again," he said. "Will you tell me where I can get at Adler?"

"It would be easier to tell you where a hawk lives," answered Swain. "Adler has been seen around these mountains, from time to time, the way you see hawks in the sky, but no one knows where he lives."

"You can go back," said Barney. "There's nothing that you can do here. I'm sorry I bothered you." He broke off to groan: "She must have suspected him all the time. That was why she seemed cold; that was why she seemed to be thinking of something else all the while!"

"I can go back to Coffeeville and spread the alarm," said Swain. "But if Adler has turned his hand to kidnapping, no one knows what a close hunt will make him do. I'm going back, Dwyer, and give word to the sheriff. And in the meantime, if there's ever a thing I can do for you, let me know. Call on me!"

Barney Dwyer, still in a trance of misery, watched the huge doctor ride away. The red mare, sniffing at something at the edge of the road, brought him to her, gloomily, his head bent in despair. It was that very dropping of his head that enabled him to see the dim outline of a very small hoof. Only a mule could have left that narrow sign.

He ran straight across the road. On the farther side were many rocks. Among them he searched, patiently for nearly an hour until, just beyond the rocks, in a patch where no pine needles lay, he found two more footprints, like the first one. And near them was the tread of a horse.

He fled through the woods along that line. With rattling bit chains and jouncing stirrups, the mare followed him, until he saw a small glint of white on the tip of the lowest branch of a pine tree. It was a very small segment of white cloth, about the texture of a handkerchief, a woman's handkerchief.

He held it gingerly on the tips of his fingers. Was it hers? Had she ripped up the handkerchief and left this spot of white as a mark for a turning point, perhaps, on the trail? He knew there was about Sue always a thin fragrance of lavendar. But when he tried to find that perfume on this shred of cloth, all he was aware of was the sweating of the mare close by and the keen, pure odor of the pines.

He went on in the first direction, came to open ground, and found no sign at all. He doubled back to the place where the white shred of cloth had been found, and searching to the right, he located the hoofprints almost instantly.

That settled it in the mind of Barney Dwyer. It was the trail of the old man and the girl. Helpless as he had seemed, Doc Adler must have had a horse and a mule at close hand, and he had taken the girl away at the very time when McGregor and young Peary were chasing Barney through the trees and over the hills toward Coffeeville. But as she was carried off, she had known how to blaze the trail behind her.

Here Barney closed his eyes and threw back his head with a silent prayer for more cunning on the trail. Then he started forward again.

He rode the mare now, in order to cover the way more rapidly, stooping low from the saddle to scan the ground.

That was how he happened to find the second little white marker, like a pale dot on the leaves.

He scooped it up without dismounting, and found, to be sure, that it was of exactly the same texture as the first bit. So he abandoned the straight line of the trails and again cut for sign. And this time he found it to the left, where the riders had passed down a long, close avenue of trees, straight as a gun barrel, with a blazing eye of sun at the farther end.

So Barney rode swiftly down that natural street and into the open day again. He was on a long, naked sweep of rock, but through a crevice grew up a few bushes. On one of these he saw from a distance the thin gleam of a patch of white.

It was another fragment of the same cloth. An exultation mastered Barney Dwyer. Nothing in his life compared with the wordless appeal of those ragged little bits of white.

This one pointed him down into the valley, so he descended at once to the bottom, where the stream ran bright as polished silver. It was very shallow. The trail crossed and recrossed it.

It was a beautiful valley, with wild, precipitous sides, sometimes of sheer rock, sometimes with projecting shoulders covered with trees. On the tops of the cliffs the dark fringe of the forest began again, with the pale mountain summits rising behind.

He felt that he could ride almost blindly down this narrow valley, picking up the sign of the fugitives only now and again. However many people had ridden the trail before, the ravine seemed empty now. And if Adler were likened to a hawk, then he must have carried Sue off to some aerie in the higher mountains. So Barney made good time, swinging the mare along at a full gallop.

That was how he almost ran into the arms of danger. For rounding a bend just after he had forded the stream for the tenth time, he saw the shadowy forms of riders coming toward him behind trees.

He jumped the mare into a great, green bower that covered them both like a wave of the sea, and, peering out from this, he saw Sheriff Elder and five other riders come streaming around the bend, six grim men on six strong horses, and every man with a rifle laid across his saddle fork.

They came on softly. The wind covered the noise of their horses and not a one of them spoke until they reached the verge of the water through which Barney had just passed.

Then the sheriff halted them all by the lifting of his hand. Barney could hear him speaking.

"Justis," said the sheriff, "take Walker and Harmon and go up along the rimrock. Hunt every crack in the rock to the bottom. Because I've got the feeling in my bones that they're somewhere around here."

"Who d'you want the most, Elder?" asked the man named Justis.

"I've got a private grudge against Barney Dwyer," said the sheriff, "but that's not why I've turned a hundred men loose hunting through the mountains. It isn't what I want to find, but what the law wants to find. And the law wants McGregor and that murdering young Len Peary!"

The party split at once into two bits. Three men turned sharply to the side and started up the slope toward the valley wall. The sheriff and two more of his crew continued down the valley trail.

But Barney remained quivering like a hunted deer long after they were all out of sight.

A hundred men! Thirty-five parties of three—all armed men—all hunting for scalps through the mountains like so many groups of red Indians! And he, Barney Dwyer, had no weapons in his hands! It was as though he were attempting to handle red-hot coals without so much as leather gloves to protect his skin.

He went out from his covert again. The valley no longer was, to him, an empty place, but rather it was trembling with danger. Out of every shadow he expected a rifle to speak.

He was on tiptoe with tension when he saw another rider canter from a copse a quarter of a mile ahead of him on a horse darkly polished with sweat. And, by something gallant and adventurous in the bearing, he knew that it was Leonard Peary. The woods beside the creek received Peary and covered him, and Barney was instantly after him.

What person other than Len Peary had a motive in stealing the girl? Might not that sinister Doc Adler have acted as his

agent? Barney rushed the mare in pursuit as rashly as though
he could afford to despise rifle bullets.

He came to the very spot where the trees had covered the
shining horse of Peary. It was a narrow strip. Through the tree
trunks he could see the brightness of the water. So he
dismounted and went through as soundlessly as a gliding
snake.

He came out on the bank. He saw where the prints of the
hoofs of a horse had rounded the side of the stream and gone
down to the water, but of horse and of man, all traces had
disappeared. Len Peary and his mustang had vanished like a
thought.

Barney lifted his eyes with despair. For on the other side of
the creek, across which Peary might have passed with his
horse, there was nothing but a vast wall of rubble and of solid
rock that lifted up to a square-topped mesa. Only one tree
grew at the base of the rock, leaning its huge trunk and
branches out over the stream, but all the rest of the stone wall
was impregnable, incapable of giving refuge. Barney felt a
darkness of wonder rush over his brain.

18

The top of that rocky mesa was several acres in extent and it
was as pleasant as a garden. It was a gently hollowed basin
with a break in the side toward the creek below. Ancient trees
stood on that unspoiled ground, and grass thick as a lawn. A
gray mule and a herd of three goats strolled on that grass, and
under a dappling of shadow moved some sheep, close together, like a drifting of cirrus clouds.

The mesa rose well above the bottom of the valley, yet a
spring leaped in the center of the green hollow, ran down into
a spacious pool, and then trickled away over the lip of the
cliff toward the creek beneath. And where the pool widened,

stood a small log cabin, very roughly built, with McGregor and Doc Adler and Susan Jones seated in homemade chairs before it. The sun was far enough to the west to throw the shadow of the house over the group, and therefore they were at ease, Adler sucking at a pipe, McGregor with a cigarette, and the girl leaning well back, with both hands cupped under her head. A little woolly, mongrel dog that looked like an undergrown sheep was curled up between the feet of Adler.

"And trout, too," old Adler was saying. "I've hooked trout out of it, too! You can call me a liar, but doggone me if I ain't hooked trout out of that there pool, and cooked them, and ate them, too."

The small dog wakened from sleep, jumped up, and trotted busily off to the edge of the mesa.

"What's your dog going after?" asked McGregor.

"He's goin' the rounds," said Doc Adler. "He's got nerves, is what he's got. That Sammy dog, he likes to be up here high in the air, but he don't want no guests along with him. He's kind of a snob. He's the kind of a snob that would lick a gentleman's hand and bite a tramp in the pants. So he goes the rounds, now and then, and mostly he watches to see that nobody can be comin' up the trail."

"What would come up the trail?" asked McGregor.

"Well," said Doc Adler, "the facts is, Mack, that there's a lot of folks that would like to cut my throat to see whether my blood was red or blue or green, maybe. And Sammy seems to know that trouble ain't never so very far away. Him and me, Mack, we keep peerin' around to see what might come over the edge of the sky."

McGregor turned his dull eyes upon the old man.

"It's a lonely life," said he. "I wouldn't like to be leading it at your age."

"You ain't gonna be leading it at my age," answered Adler. "Because you ain't gunna be alive at my age. You got too much enthusiasm in you, Mack, to live this long. But it ain't so lonely, for me. I got my memories. I'd rather have a lot of my memories than a whole flock of sons and grandsons around me."

"They'd be spending your money, Doc. Is that it?" asked McGregor.

"Money?" snapped Adler. "And what would I be doin' with money, Mack? You're talkin' like a fool! Money? What would money mean to me, roostin' up here like an old buzzard on a rock?"

McGregor smiled, and turned his eyes away. He said nothing, but it was plain that his mind had not left the subject.

The girl stood up.

"Tell me a story about myself," she said.

"I'll tell you a story," said Doc Adler. "It goes like this: Susan was a good little girl. She never done nothin' wrong, and she always helped her ma around the house. So what d'you think became of this good little girl? Why, she went and got fond of a fat-faced fool of a half-wit, by the name of Barney Dwyer, and she got herself clean mired down in trouble, was what she got herself, till finally she found herself setting up on the top of a mesa and never knowin' how she got there, hardly, and every minute she set there, Barney Dwyer was sure comin' closer and closer until—"

"Stop it, Doc,'" advised McGregor, "or you'll drive her crazy. What's the matter with that dog?"

For Sammy the mongrel had turned from the edge of the mesa and bolted toward the cabin at full speed. His tail was tucked between his legs. It was wonderful to see his fear and to notice his silence, in spite of it.

"He's seen something!" declared Adler, jumping to his feet. "There's something coming up the trail, It may be a coyote—or it may be a whole doggone posse, for all that I know. I'll go see."

He stretched his long legs to cross the little plateau while Sammy, instead of following, crouched before the feet of McGregor. The latter stretched out his hand toward the girl, and she got up instantly and stood beside him, saying, "I'll follow you. I won't try to bolt or to yell. But don't touch me, Mack!"

"I'm poison to you, am I?" he asked her.

"You're poison to the whole world," she told him, in

answer. She stared evenly back at him. "I'd rather touch a snake than you, Mack."

Before he could answer, they saw old Adler turn suddenly toward them from the edge of the mesa. He ran back with a shambling stride, making a signal for them to retreat.

McGregor caught up two of the chairs and placed them inside the door of the cabin.

"We've got to dip into the tunnel, Sue," he commanded, urging her back from the main room of the little house to the storage shed that opened behind it.

She obeyed, but there was a tremor of excitement in her as she heard a horse whinny not far away.

The whole floor of the house was the clean, dry limestone that composed the mesa. It was scored across by many deep cracks, and under the edge of one of these crevices, McGregor fitted the tips of his fingers, and lifted. A whole slab of the stone gave way a little, commenced to resist the pressure, and then stuck fast.

McGregor grunted with effort and with surprise.

"It's as if somebody were holding it down!" he exclaimed. He gave a great heave. The stone merely shuddered, and as he stopped pulling, it settled back in place with a jerk.

It was a face polished with sweat that McGregor turned to the girl.

"It's stuck—something's wrong with it!" he muttered.

The footfall of old Adler entered the front of the cabin.

"Are you safe down, McGregor?" he called in a subdued voice, as though others were near who might overhear him.

"The damned top stone is stuck," said McGregor, hurrying back into the front room, his hand on the arm of the girl to keep her with him. "What d'you do about that?"

"Stuck?" snarled Doc Adler. "You fool, it can't be stuck —it—"

Out the door, Sue Jones saw what seemed to her the most beautiful sight in the world—Sheriff Elder and five men coming straight toward the cabin, on foot, each with a long rifle in his hand.

"The attic?" said McGregor. "Or shall we fight 'em, Doc?"

"Fight 'em? Two agin six? Up that ladder into the attic. Quick!"

"And be trapped? I'll never take a step to the attic!" exclaimed McGregor.

"Then let 'em catch you here!" said Adler. "You've bungled everything. I never wanted to take you here. But *they* won't bungle things—not when they tie a rope around your neck and hang you up, McGregor! You know what they'll do when they see the girl and learn the yarn she can spin. Get up that ladder—and I'll try to keep 'em from follerin'!"

McGregor looked wildly, desperately around him, for a moment. Then he waved the girl before him. Up she went, scurrying. McGregor followed. And as they entered the darkness of the attic, old Adler removed the ladder from the open trap, and laid it against the side of the wall, flat on the limestone floor. McGregor lowered the trap; a redoubled darkness poured over the eyes of the girl.

19

It was not a total darkness, however, that covered Sue. Small dim slits and eyes of light appeared on the floor of the attic, and lying flat, she put her eye to the largest gap and found that almost the whole of the main room was instantly in view.

Beside her, the whisper of McGregor sounded.

"If you make a sound, if you make a move to attract 'em, Sue—if you so much as knock some dust through one of the cracks . . . I'll finish you before they have a chance to finish me. You've been wrecking my whole game for me. You've been pulling Len Peary away from me. It's on account of you that Dwyer is on my trail. And now you'll pay for it, woman or no woman, if they corner me with you here."

The whisper ended. And she knew perfectly that he meant

what he said. He had merely laid one finger on her arm, but it was like the touch of steel, hard, relentless, heavy.

So she lay still, waiting, watching. One cry from her and the six men who were approaching the cabin would tear it to shreds to find her. But they would only find her dead body. Her prayer must be that her friends would fail in their search.

Old Doc Adler had gone to the door of the cabin, and he could be seen waving toward the strangers.

"Hello, boys," said Adler. "Hello, Sheriff. Mighty glad to see you, Elder. Got anything framed up on me, today?"

"I've found out your hiding place, have I?" said Sheriff Elder. "And I think I'll be taking you out of this, Adler. I think it's jail for you, now!"

"All right," said Adler. "There's plenty of things that I could be stuck in jail for. What have you run down at last, Elder?"

He backed away from the door, inviting the others to enter. Elder came striding in with the long-haired frontiersman, Justis, behind him. Two more of the men entered. Then the sheriff commanded: "Start hunting, boys. I'll stay here and talk to this old toothless mountain lion while you're working the ground over. Sit down, Adler. Wait a minute. I'll see if you have any guns around you."

The posse scattered, as Adler answered: "No guns, Elder. No, sir, I ain't much good with guns no more."

"Why not?" asked the sheriff. "Your hands are steady enough."

"My hands are steady, but my eyes ain't no good, no more. I've got a knife on me, and that's all."

"Let me have it, then. Never mind, I'll find it."

The dexterous and familiar hands of the sheriff hunted through the clothes of Adler and produced from them, in fact, only one long, murderously sharp Bowie knife. Elder felt the edge of it and nodded.

"That would cut a throat, eh?" said he.

"And maybe it has, Sheriff," answered Adler. "You can't tell. Maybe it *has* cut a throat or two. You take a look and you'll see that it's been sharpened and sharpened, and wore

down and wore down. Not all by skinnin' rabbits and coyotes, neither!''

He sat down facing the sheriff and began to rub his claws
together, laughing. With all her heart the girl wondered at that
evil old face, for she felt that Doc Adler was almost welcom-
ing the danger of that search.

"We've had word out of Coffeeville that may wipe the grin
off your face," said the sheriff. "What's become of the girl,
Adler? Answer me that!''

"What girl?'' asked Adler.

The sheriff looked coldly at him for a long moment.
"Lying won't help you a lot," he said finally. "The girl you
were with today. Sue Jones is her name.''

"Her that give me the hand when I was down and out?''
said Adler. "Is that the one you mean?''

"Go on,'' said the sheriff curtly.

"Why,'' said the old villain, "she's back yonder in the
pine trees, waitin' for Barney Dwyer, unless he's come and
fetched her along to Coffeeville by this time.''

"What happened?'' asked the sheriff.

"I'm gettin' old,'' answered Adler, "and the way of it was
that as I was riding my old gray mule along the Coffeeville
road, I got dizzy. And I climbed off that mule and started to
walk, waitin' for my head to clear. But it didn't clear. No, sir,
it just got more clouded over, and the first thing I knew,
somebody had picked me up off of the ground, where I must
of fainted, maybe. It was Barney Dwyer and the girl. I was
considerable weak. Dwyer went off to fetch a doctor from
Coffeeville, but after a few minutes I felt better, by a whole
pile, and so I just told the girl that I could fend for myself,
now, and I went off and found the mule in the trees, and rode
back home. That's all.''

"And the girl?'' said the sheriff, snapping out the words.

"She tried to keep me from goin' off,'' said Adler. "There's
a lot of kindness and goodness in that girl, Sheriff. She
wanted me to stay till a doctor came. But bein' my age, I
don't want no doctor listening to see is there a leak in my
heart, or is my liver goin' back on me. No, sir, I don't want
to start dyin' of fear before I'm dyin' in fact. Y'understand?''

"Adler," said the sheriff, gravely, "that girl was gone when Dwyer brought the doctor back."

"Hold on!" exclaimed Adler. "What would of happened to her, then?"

The sheriff raised a forefinger as he continued: "How many murders and robberies you've chalked up to your credit, Adler, I don't know. But if you've had a hand in making that girl disappear I'm going to make you sweat in hell for it. That is, unless you can turn her up for us. You hear me? Find the girl for us, and no harm done to her, and we'll call the deal square and forget bygones."

"Wait a minute," said Adler, frowning. "Who would of laid a finger on her? Who would of wanted to? Folks don't bother women. Not in this part of the world they don't, and you know it! Any girl could ride from one end of the Rockies to the other, and no harm ever come to her. You know that, too!"

The sheriff leaned forward, peering earnestly into that long, chalky, evil face. But Adler was wearing an expression of the most open candor.

He even added: "I'll tell you what, Sheriff. If anything's happened to that girl, I'm gunna stir my stumps to find out who bothered her. But it ain't likely that nobody bothered her. She just got tired of waitin' for Dwyer and she went to meet him on the way back, after I rode off. That's what happened, sure."

"I think you're lying, Adler,' said the sheriff, "and God help you if there's any proof of it!"

Justis appeared in the doorway.

"We've gone over the whole doggone mesa," he said. "We don't find no sign of her. We've found some sheep and goats and a mule. That's all."

"What you find in the shed?" asked the sheriff.

"All kinds of groceries and provisions. Adler has enough chuck in there to feed him for a couple years," said Justis.

"Nothing else?"

"Yeah. Some furs and pelts. And some old traps. And some saddles and—"

"I don't care about that stuff," said the sheriff. "But I

want to know a lot of other things. I want to know why that
trail up the face of the mesa isn't worn more. Adler's been
here a long time, but it took a microscope, almost, to find
any sign of a trail over the rocks. We were only guessing,
when we left the horses down below and climbed up to the
top of the rock.''

"The trail ain't wore deep," said Adler, "because it ain't
often that I leave here and take a ride. I'm an old man,
Sheriff, and when a gent gets old, he likes to set quiet and
smell the wind, and feel the sun, and let the days go by.''

He shook his head slowly from side to side, as he spoke.

"Have you looked everywhere?" asked the sheriff.

Justis raised his head and stared at the trapdoor in the
ceiling; then glanced down toward the ladder that was laid
along the wall.

But before the deputy could speak, Adler himself had said:
"You ain't had a peek into the attic, yet. Better see if
anything's up there!''

At that, Sue's whole body trembled violently. And McGregor
gripped her arm.

She felt that she would stifle. It seemed that the air had lost
all its oxygen.

"That's true," said the sheriff. "Lay the ladder against the
hole, up there, Justis. What's in the attic, Adler?''

"Dust," said Adler.

Justis raised the length of the clumsy ladder, and fitted it in
place on the floor.

"Nothing up there at all, eh?" repeated the sheriff.

"Not that I know of," said Adler. "But maybe I'm wrong.
There might be a whole string of bats up there; there might be
a mountain lion, for all I know, and a whole litter of cubs. I
ain't been up there for years. I dunno what you'll find!''

He chuckled a little and made a gesture with the palm of
his hand turned up, as though offering them free inspection of
all of his possessions.

"Climb up there and move the trapdoor," said the sheriff
to Justis. "Be ready to shoot, too.''

Justis climbed up the ladder and pressed with one hand at
the trapdoor; and at the same time McGregor softly scraped a

quantity of dust over the crack just above the face of the deputy.

It sifted through and fell into his eyes and nose.

He clung to the ladder, shaking it with a fit of coughing. Then he retreated, slowly, still gasping.

"Dust!" he said. "There ain't nothing but dust up there— and old Adler told the truth, for once."

"Better open that trap," said the sheriff. "I'll do it myself. We've got to make sure."

"Ain't we made sure already?" asked Justis, with irritation, "or maybe I've just gone and blinded myself for nothin'! If that trapdoor had been lifted any time recent, would there be such a pile of dust on it? Look there, how it's still falling since I shook that trapdoor?"

The sheriff screened his eyes and stared up. It seemed to Sue Jones that he was looking straight into her face, that he must see her clearly, so perfectly could she survey him.

But then he shook his head.

"You're right, Justis," said he. "We'll keep on searching a while, anyway. And if we can't take anything else away from this place, we can take Adler and let him smell the inside of a jail once more!"

20

Barney, when he reached the bank of the stream and found no sign of Peary before him, but only that blank wall of limestone, with the one big tree lodged in it close above the water, continued to stare for a long time in simple inability to understand the nature of the miracle that could have snatched Peary away.

For Len Peary could not have ridden up the bank or down it without making a loud sound of crashing through the underbrush. He must have advanced into the stream, then—but could a man and a horse simply dissolve there? And how could they be carried away by a rush of water that was hardly more than two feet deep at the deepest?

He was so interested in the problem, that he kept on staring long after he had the slightest real expectation of solving the mystery. And it was this length of idle examination that at last showed him a little eye of white on one of the outer leaves of the tree across the creek.

Ordinarily, it would have meant nothing to him, but he had been seeing too many similar little white patches, on the trail, and therefore, on glimpse of this new one, he pressed straight on into the current until he came to the tree. It stood out on the strength of the sweeping water. There was a deeper pool, here, with only a swirling eddy in it. And on an outer leaf he picked off just such a wisp of cloth as he had found before.

His amazement increased. At last, pushing back the branch of the tree that was nearest to him, he looked under it and saw the green reflections deep in the water, with the slow whirl of the eddy ruffling them.

He could see how the tree was moored to the shore, now. For at the very base of the limestone cliff there was a small apron of detritus that spilled out into the stream, and in and over this skirting of soil arose the great roots of the tree. It was lifting like a spider on eight immense legs.

Between the branches and the water there was a low, cool green cavern, into which the mare advanced cautiously, snuffing at the air and plainly ill at ease. Then, pausing, she shook her head in positive fear. She began to back up, eyeing the dark arch that extended under one of the largest roots. So Barney idly leaned from the saddle, and to his amazement he was able to look a considerable distance under that root into what seemed a tunnel sunk in the vitals of the stone.

He came closer.

If he leaned flat forward in the saddle, it was possible for him to pass under the height of the arching root without any difficulty, and, in a moment, he stood with the mare, in a long, narrow cavern.

It was an amazing place, to Barney. When he turned and glanced back, he could see the green shimmering of the shadow of the tree that the strength of the sun cast brightly upon the face of the creek. But that was not the only illumination of the tunnel. For at the top of it extended an irregular crevice, one of those many cracks that he had noted from the opposite bank of the stream. Through that narrow opening, he made sure of the nearer details of the cave.

It had evidently been eaten out, ages ago, by the slow action of a stream of water. Water had chiseled a tunnel, in some places ragged, in some places with hand-smoothed walls and polished ceilings.

This shaft led at a steep rate not directly up the face of the cliff, but sloping far to the right to a point where it disappeared around an elbow-bend.

But what set the heart of Barney Dwyer beating so fast was that he had seen the prints of the hoofs not of one horse, but of many, on the stone of the cave floor. And this was the perfect explanation of the manner in which Peary had disappeared.

Since he could not guess what lay before him, he abandoned the mare at the entrance to the tunnel, tethering her to a massive fragment that had fallen from the roof to the floor. When he left her she whinnied after him, but no louder than a whisper, and when he turned back to her in an agony of apprehension, and made gestures, she seemed to know at once what he meant. She remained silent, her ears straining forward, the quivering green reflection from the surface of the creek playing over her in rapid vibrations.

Suppose that another man should enter the cave and find her there?

Well, such things were not to be thought of. They only stole the strength from his heart before the contest and the real danger began. For if Leonard Peary were somewhere in this underground retreat, then to be sure he would have other men with him—the great McGregor, for instance?

He went on gradually and cautiously, ready to leap like a cat at the first sound. But what he heard was the stamp of a horse, and a low snuffling sound, as when a horse snorts while its muzzle is buried in forage. Then he came on an excellent stable that the work of the water had quarried out of the rock just beyond that elbow-bend in the tunnel. Here the underground currents had drilled out a wide passage, and along one side of it, where the rock floor was perfectly level, half a dozen horses were stabled.

Above the stalled horses, through a widening of the crack as through a skylight, sun and fresh air entered. It was as perfect a stable as any liveryman could have wished to establish—this one in the heart of the limestone cliff. And Barney could have stopped to admire it, at any other time. But as it was, he dropped on his hands and knees like a soundless ghost. For there was Leonard Peary, stripping the saddle and bridle from the back of a sweating horse.

He passed out of the shadow across the strong yellow ray of light, and Barney could see his face perfectly. The dark and smiling beauty of it oppressed him. How could Sue have given up a man like this in order to ride away with such a simple fellow as himself? And that was not all! Some day Peary would again find Sue, and when he stood beside her, Barney thought a force of natural magic would be sufficient to make her forget Barney Dwyer entirely, except as a subject for laughter.

Len Peary, having finished his work with the horse, stood in the full beam of the sunlight while he rolled a cigarette, which he lighted, and which sent upward a white cloud that left watermarkings of shadow upon the handsome face of Peary.

Barney, slinking low and close to the wall, came up behind the fine fellow little by little. Then one of the horses snorted and stamped with a violence that made Peary jerk about to see what might be wrong. That was how he happened to confront Barney when Dwyer was hardly a stride away.

The cigarette dashed against the wall and knocked out a shower of brilliant sparks in the shadow. The hand that had held it flashed out a revolver, while Peary leaped back and to the side to escape Barney's rush.

But he was much too close, Barney caught the revolver with his left hand and turned the muzzle away from his body. He wanted to beat the iron weight of his other fist into the face of Peary, but instead, he grasped Peary by the hair of the head and jerked him to his knees.

By chance, the yellow of the sunlight gilded the face of Peary, showed the flare of the nostrils, the maniac fear in the eyes. That picture sickened Barney and robbed him of his anger. He remembered, too, that Peary had not cried out, had not uttered a sound. Terror seemed to have gagged him from the first instant.

Both of Barney's hands relaxed their grasp; but in one of them he took away the revolver from Peary's fingers.

He stepped back. Peary did not offer to rise. He merely slumped sideways against the wall of the tunnel and dropped his head on his chest. It was as though a bullet already had crashed through his body and the life were running out of him.

"I'm not going to harm you—I guess," said Barney, and his breath was hot in his throat. "Stand up, Len."

Peary got slowly to his feet. He kept one hand on the wall for support, and his head still drooped. It was clear that shame was the bullet that had struck him.

"Len," said Barney, "you and McGregor chased me and shot at me. I expected it of him. I didn't think you'd do such a thing."

"No," said the faint voice of Peary, "you wouldn't expect that."

Barney waited. But not an excuse was offered.

"You tried to kill me, Len," he repeated.

"Yes," said Peary. "I tried to."

"Why?" asked Barney. "What have I done to you, Len, except to try to help you?"

"Nothing. You've done nothing to me," answered Peary. "But I had to have you out of the way."

Barney made a vague gesture to the side.

"It was Sue. Is that it?" he asked.

Peary nodded.

And it was Barney who said: "I'm sorry about that. But she'll see farther through me, one of these days. And then she'll forget me, and likely she'll remember you, then."

"She's seen all the way through you, already," answered

Peary, lifting his head suddenly, at last. "And she knows that you're better stuff—than the rest of us. A lot better."

"Do you know where she is now?" asked Barney, feeling that he could not answer those last words.

"Yes. I know," said Peary. He closed his eyes, opened them again, and then jerked a thumb over his shoulder. "She's here," he said.

"Where? Farther up the tunnel?"

"Clear at the top of it," said Peary. "In a cabin on top of the rock."

A groan of relief came from the throat of Barney.

"Anyone with her?" he asked.

"Yes. Adler and McGregor."

"The old man—he was Adler?"

"Yes. He was Doc Adler."

"And the whole thing was a scheme to get me away from Sue?"

Peary said nothing. His silence was a sufficient answer.

"And what do they want to happen?" asked Barney.

Finally Peary broke out: "I'll tell you! You've given me my life before. I suppose you'll give it to me again. I've been a cur. Maybe I'm a worse cur to go on talking now. But I'll tell you."

He gathered himself, with a great effort.

"They know that you'll never leave these mountains till you've found Sue. So they wait on the rock like old eagles, until they get a chance to drop on you. And once you're out of the way, then I appear, Barney. I'm to rescue Sue from 'em, d'you see? No one is to know what's become of you. She'll begin to forget you after a time, and she'll begin to be grateful to me. That's the whole way of it. McGregor evens his score against you; and I have my chance with Sue. That was the plan. And—if I were you, I'd use that gun you've got in your hand. It shoots straight!"

In the pause that followed, there was no sound except the heavy breathing of Barney Dwyer.

Then he said tersely: "Maybe I could trust you now, Len. But I'd be afraid to leave you behind me. Walk over there behind the horses, will you? I'm going to leave you tied up so you can't manage any harm while I'm gone."

Peary marched ahead and stood by the saddles and bridles that hung against the wall of the tunnel. With bridle reins, Barney tied him securely, hand and foot, and hand to foot. He took off Peary's bandana, wadded it into a tight ball, and wedged it in behind his teeth.

"Is that going to choke you, Len?" he asked with a strange concern.

Peary shook his head, and slumped back against the wall. And Barney, after staring at him a moment, went on up the angling slope of the tunnel until it grew steeper and steeper and ended against a flat slab of stone. He tried the weight of it. It lifted a little easily enough and let in on his ears the sound of voices and of hurrying steps.

21

He still had his grip on a rough ledge of the stone that closed the trap when a strong pull from above almost tore the rock away from him. Instinctively he resisted, and heard the voice of McGregor immediately above him, exclaiming in fear and astonishment.

McGregor, who could shoot as though a wizard were controlling the guns! A second pull came, but this time the iron strength of Barney secured the stone slab as firmly as mortar.

After that, he waited for a fresh attempt.

He wondered if he should retreat down the passage. He wondered if he should suddenly strive to force his way through into the cabin, which, according to Peary, stood above?

Twice, at considerable intervals, he pushed up the stone a mere trifle.

The first time, he heard the familiar voice of Sheriff Elder speaking not far away. Then tramplings came above him. Some small particles of stone showered down into his face. But that was all.

No one again attempted to lift the stone, until at last, eaten with impatience, he pushed it up once more. There was no sound for the moment. Then he heard retreating footfalls, retreating voices.

Were they leaving, the girl and the two men?

He lifted the stone still farther, and crawled out into a small storage shed surrounded with shelves and bins.

And now he heard a voice that was hardly out of his ears, it was so recent a memory—it was the sound of Doc Adler's speech, as the old man said, "All right, Mack. It's all clear. They've gone over the edge of the mesa, the sheriff and all of 'em."

Hinges creaked in the upper part of the next room.

"Sure he won't come back?" asked McGregor.

"I dunno," said Adler. "Not today, I guess. Him findin' me here, it's spoiled things for me. I've gotta move, after this, and where'll I find as snug a hole as this to lie up in? But I dunno. It was pretty high nigh worth a move—hood-winkin' the sheriff like that!"

"He might have taken you with him," said McGregor, his voice descending. "Come on, Sue. Come on down, will you?"

"I'm coming," said the voice for which Barney waited most of all. And he set his teeth, hearing it now. For he wanted to rush blindly in on them all, no matter who might be there, and rush off with Sue. He had to fight against that insane impulse.

"How'd the dust come into the face of that fellow, Justis?" asked Adler.

"I poured some through a crack right over his head," said McGregor.

Adler laughed heartily.

"You got brains, is what you got, Mack," said he.

Barney leveled his revolver at the open door between the shed and the main body of the cabin, and then he crept closer.

"Come along, Sue," said McGregor.

"I'll stay in here, Mack," she said. "I'm sick of the faces of you two."

"You'll have a change of scene when the half-wit comes along," sneered McGregor. "He'll brighten things up a good deal for you, Sue."

She made no answer.

Adler's voice sounded from the distance: "Comin', Mack?"

"Come along, Sue!" exclaimed McGregor. "D'you think that I'll leave you alone here?"

"I might slip away down the trap and through the tunnel, eh?" she said. "Well, all right."

Then Barney stepped into the open doorway, and saw McGregor squarely facing him in the outer door. Those two hands of Big Mack started for guns and paused in mid-gesture.

"Don't move, McGregor!" said Barney. "Be like a stone! Don't move!"

And McGregor did not move. He was admirable in the crisis. Not a muscle of his face stirred to betray fear; not a touch of pallor turned his swarthy skin pale.

"All right, Barney; all right, my lad," said he. "You have a handful of aces, again. It's your turn, Barney."

Barney dared not glance aside at the girl, though all his soul was urging him to look at her. She was a presence that he felt, not one that he saw.

She was coming toward him. She had not cried out. She had not uttered a sound.

"What'll I do with him?" asked Barney.

She answered rapidly: "You can't do murder, Barney. Make him step back inside."

"Oh, Mack! Mack!" called the voice of old Adler from the distance. "I want you to see—"

The rest of those words Barney did not hear.

"Come in," said Barney to McGregor.

And McGregor stepped through the doorway. The girl was instantly behind him and pulled the door shut. Then her rapid hands filched his two guns.

"Can we take him with us?" she asked.

"Where, Sue?" asked Barney, frowning with doubt. "What could we do with him? Where could we take him?"

"To a sheriff," said the girl. "There's a crime to charge against him now. I've heard him talk here of a good many things, Barney. They only want a ghost of an excuse to put him in prison until his head is white, and we have plenty of charges against him now!"

"But if we take him," argued Barney, "you know that the sheriff wants me, also?"

"What's against you compared with what's against Mc-Gregor?" said the girl. "Why, they'll worship you, Barney, if you can bring him in. Quick! Here's twine—it's better than rope to hold his hands. I'll do it. Never mind. Only watch him!"

McGregor made no resistance. He let himself be tied like a sheep. Neither did he speak a word, but his eyes burned like an acid into the face of Barney Dwyer.

The situation might be reversed again, and if the time came, Barney could guess how short would be his shrift. There would be no nonsense on the part of McGregor about murder or no murder.

When those formidable hands were tied, Barney could look for the first time at the girl, and she at him. They spared one golden second for that glance, and then they herded the prisoner into the storage room.

"Mack!" yelled the angry voice of old Adler, drawing nearer. "What's the idea of the closed door?"

Barney lifted the stone trap. Into the aperture, McGregor got down at once. The girl followed, weighted down by the burden of the two big Colts. Barney was last. He closed the trap behind him, and so they hurried down the passage to the subterranean stables.

They were almost at the place when they heard a noise behind them, and then the piercing voice of Adler, shouting: "Mack!"

"Here!" thundered McGregor in answer. "Here, and caught by Dwyer!"

22

It was as though there had been loosed after them a river of fire to rush down the tunnel; it was as though all the path they might follow outside of the cave were sown with explosives. Barney Dwyer caught big McGregor by the shoulder and jerked him against the wall. The shock of the meeting between flesh and rock made the eyes stagger in the head of McGregor, but he merely sneered at Barney.

"Now your brains against Adler's brains," he said. "And see who wins through to Coffeeville!"

That was it. Their brains against the brains of that lean, devilish old wolf, Adler.

There were six horses there in the underground stables. They hustled saddles onto five of them. The one that had just been brought back by Len Peary seemed too spent to be of much use to friend or to enemy as it stood hanging its head, refusing to eat. Five saddles were more than they needed for their party of four, to be sure; and there was the red mare waiting for her master at the side of the river. But in case they might need to change horses on the way, they might not have time to change saddles at the same time.

With the saddled horses, they went on, McGregor and Len Peary herded in front, and the horses following.

Up to that time, there had not been many words exchanged. The girl had simple said to Peary: "Well, this is the way of it, is it? You were in the whole game from the first, were you? You're not a traitor! You're not even a man!"

Peary had no answer to make to that. From the moment when Barney had mastered him, in fact, there had seemed little or no life in him. He went on like a dead thing. He looked down at his feet, never at the girl. And Barney had

said to her: "Easy, Sue! Don't be too hard on him. You don't
know—"

"I don't know what?" she asked savagely.

"You don't know how much he loves you," said Barney.
She gave Barney such a bitter glance that he was afraid her
wrath would descend even upon *his* devoted head, after that;
but she said not a word more.

They got down to the mouth of the tunnel, and there they
saw the quivering green reflection from the surface of the
stream outside. They saw the mare standing there, made
trembling and unreal in the strange light.

Peary said a thing that never died out of the mind of
Barney in time to come. He said to McGregor: "You see how
it is, Mack. Even horses—even the dumb beasts—are more
faithful to honest men!"

Mack answered with his dark sneer: "Dumb beasts understand dumb fools better. That's all!"

At the entrance to the long tunnel, Barney made McGregor
and Peary mount. He tied their horses bit to bit by a length of
rope, the end of which was fastened to the saddle of the red
mare.

Then he said: "McGregor, and Len, you see how things
are. It happens that I have guns, and you haven't. Also, your
hands are tied. If you try to get away, if you try any tricks, I
wouldn't like to shoot, but I'd have to! Now ride out into the
water, please. Don't shout. Don't call out. Doc Adler might
be watching for us from the top of the rock!"

That was the fear, of course. And from the top of the mesa
a rifleman might have done terrible execution as they rushed
the horses across the narrow little creek. But there was no
firing above them. They got peaceably across and into the
brush on the farther side. When they looked back, it seemed
to Barney that it was no longer a blank wall of stone but a
great, evil fortress that stood there in the middle of the
valley.

But no rifles were fired after them; they escaped into the
cloud of green. When they were shut in by the woods,
Barney said: "What shall we do now, Sue?"

"We'll head back for Coffeeville, of course," said she. "We've got a double cargo to deliver there."

She looked to Peary when she spoke about the "double" cargo. Barney wondered at her more than a little. He would have said, seeing the calm and the brightness of her, that she was on a jolly outing with dear friends, not with the terrible danger of all McGregor's men between her and safety.

"The straight way is down the valley," said Barney. "But if we go that way, won't Adler be able to signal to some of the men of McGregor's party? They're still out in the mountains, searching for their chief, don't you imagine? And perhaps Adler may know where to find them?"

Sue regarded him as one might look at a page of writing in an unknown language, and big McGregor said: "Yes, you can all see that there's a brain in that head, after all."

Barney flushed. He looked guiltily at the girl, expecting contempt or a reproof, but she merely answered: "Yes, Barney, I suppose there's still some danger ahead of us. At least, we're not exactly the same as at home. I wasn't thinking of taking the shortest cut back to Coffeeville, but I thought that we'd go back over the hills to the south. Does that suit you?"

He answered hastily, humbly: "Of course, Sue. Whatever you say will be for the best."

"Then we'll head down the valley and throw a loop around the mesa, and then cut to the south down one of the other ravines. Start along, Barney."

He had the horses of the prisoners anchored to the saddle of the red mare. Sue had the two spare lead horses tied to her mount, which was a long, low, powerfully built gray gelding. It was a curious color—black spots on a rather yellowish field. Barney got the leading trio in motion at a canter. At an easy lope they passed down the ravine, until they were well below the mesa. Then they turned to the left into the throat of a narrow gorge.

McGregor said: "It would be easy, Dwyer. One good man with a rifle could pick off all four of us. One good man could lie up in the rocks and cut us all down before we found any sign of cover."

Barney answered him, gently: "I know how you feel, Mack. I'm sorry about you, in a way, too. You've tried to do some pretty bad things to me and to Sue, too. But I wouldn't take you to the law. I wouldn't, except that we'd be afraid to let you remain loose."

The girl was well behind by this time, urging her laggard troop along, for horses with empty saddles are apt to go more negligently and carelessly ahead than horses with human burdens. Of Barney's trio, Leonard Peary was the laggard. He had the sick face of a man who is nauseated. He leaned over the horn of the saddle, and gave himself up to the darkness of his thoughts. So Barney was left practically alone with McGregor who did his part in keeping his brown horse up with the mare. He had a pair of spurs with sharp steel rowels, and a touch of them now and then would make the brown dance. Still, it was admirable to see the manner in which McGregor kept his seat, though with hands tied behind him. He was a master horseman.

Barney, full of that admiration, burst out finally: "McGregor, what made you do it?"

"Do what?" asked McGregor calmly.

"Go crooked," said Barney. "You could be anything that you want. You have a good mind. You could be anything. What made you go in for crime?"

McGregor's eyes turned dull and dark. Then he said: "If you wanted to catch fish, would you stay ashore or go to sea in a boat?"

"I'd go in a boat," said Barney, opening his round, blue eyes.

"If you wanted to find gold, would you hunt for pebbles, or dig in the rocks?"

"I'd dig in the rocks," said Barney.

"And if you wanted to find a criminal," said McGregor, "would you stay among honest men, doing honest work, or would you mix around with the crooks?"

"Are *you* trying to find someone?" asked Barney.

"My brother," said McGregor tersely. And he looked away and threw back his head with a gesture of defiance.

"Your brother!" sighed Barney Dwyer. "I never had a

brother, McGregor. And you've lost yours? Will you tell me about him?"

"There's nothing to tell," said McGregor, "except that I loved him, and while I was still a youngster, he went wrong. He disappeared. He'd killed a man, Barney."

With a lowered voice McGregor told of this, and added: "I made up my mind that when I got out in the world I'd hunt for him, and keep on hunting till I found him. So when I was able, I followed right out into his own world, and that was the world of crime, d'you see?"

"I see," said Barney, crushed with awe. "It's a great thing that you've tried to do, Mack!"

McGregor shrugged his shoulders and frowned as a man who would be pleased to shut off a conversation.

"Have you ever seen him, Mack?" asked Barney eagerly.

"Three times," said McGregor. "Once behind the bars, and once through a window as he ran past, and once in a crowd."

"And what happened every time?" asked Barney.

"I managed to set levers working that got him out of the jail—he was about to be sentenced to death. But he disappeared before I could see him. So he did in the crowd, and when he ran past the window."

"But, Mack, does he know that you're looking for him?"

"He does," said McGregor, "but he's a stern man. He feels no pull of blood, as I feel it. It'll be nothing to him when he hears that they've strung me up by the nape of the neck!"

"They won't string you up," cried out Barney.

"No? And what'll stop 'em, Dwyer?"

"*I'll* stop them," exclaimed Barney, "because I won't let them. I won't take you in. I'm going to turn you loose, McGregor, now, and I'll be your friend. I'll help you all I can to find your brother again!"

He checked the horses. A fire of enthusiasm was in his face as the girl came up to them.

"What's the matter, Barney?" she asked.

"It's about McGregor," said Barney. "We've been terribly wrong about him, and now he's told me the truth."

"He couldn't," said the girl. "The truth would burn through the leather of his own tongue."

"Ah, that's what I thought, but we didn't understand!" said Barney. "The truth is that he's gone into a criminal life just in order to find a brother who went crooked when Mack was a boy."

Sue Jones broke into ringing, cheerful laughter. To the amazement of Barney, McGregor joined the mirth, on a deeper key, and even Peary was able to summon up a wan smile.

Barney looked from face to face, totally bewildered.

"I don't understand!" said he.

The girl stopped laughing. Her amusement had actually brought a moisture into her eyes.

"Why, it's all a silly lie, Barney," said Susan Jones. "Don't you even see through that? It's just a lie, Barney, that even a child—"

She checked herself sharply. Barney, with a sigh, turned the head of the red mare up the trail again. Sue had been about to say that even a child could see through more than he was able to understand about people. And now Sue would begin to despise him!

He looked wistfully back to her as they came out of the narrows of that canyon into a broader valley, and as he looked back, the girl waved cheerfully at him.

McGregor cut into his thoughts, saying: "She'll be through with you before long. She's bound to be. Already she knows that you're nine-tenths a fool. She laughs at you today; she'll leave you tomorrow!"

"Why did you lie to me, McGregor?" he asked.

"Why," said the other, "I knew that you were a fool, but I didn't know how *big* a fool. I thought that I'd find out—and I did. The biggest fool that I've ever found in my life!"

A hollow, gloomy voice cut in upon them. It was Peary, who was saying, "You know that you lie, Mack. If he's a fool, how does he happen to have you an' me tied like a pair of pigs going to market? Because there's more heart and nerve in him than in both of us, multiplied by twenty. That's the reason. You know it, too. You're simply talking to hurt him as much as you can. It's a cowardly trick on your part."

"Is it?" exclaimed McGregor. "Are *you* turning yellow, Peary, and trying to curry favor?"

"I'm currying no favor," said young Peary. "I know what's ahead of me. And I tell you what, Mack—I'd rather hang, as I see it now, than to keep on with you."

"Ride! Ride!" shouted the girl, suddenly, from behind.

And to give a point to her words, a crackling rifle fire broke out to the side of the valley. Bullets began to hum about them. And looking back, Barney saw seven riders rushing their horses down the slope.

23

"Ride! Ride!" the girl was crying, spurring her own horse ahead. "They're McGregor's men! I recognize Pete Waller by his mustang. Ride for your life, Barney!"

Barney was already struggling forward. But as the red mare galloped more and more strongly, the two lead horses pulled back and neutralized a significant part of that effort.

Sue turned loose the pair that were on her lead rope. She rushed on the others, swinging her quirt, and slashed them across the hips until the whole party was suddenly rushing away at full speed, every horse doing his best. The red mare swung easily along in front of the rest, keeping the lead rope always taut!

But the firing stopped. The seven riders, having missed their first, distant, volley, had put their guns back in holsters and were giving their entire attention to the riding.

How had they come to this place? The sight of one among them was the convincing answer. That was a form like a gaunt old ape, bowing over the neck of the fastest of the horses. And as the wind furled the brim of his hat, Barney saw the flash of his silver hair. It was old Doc Adler again!

He must have guessed their probable course of retreat, and leaving the mesa instantly, sped across country to get to McGregor's distant men. So well had he guessed, that if Barney had delayed another minute of time on the way, the valley would have been blocked. The volley that began the battle would have ended it. But by the grace of a few seconds, Adler brought up those fighting men only in time to see the prey already slipping through the trap.

They were picked horses that the four were sitting upon. But two of them were riding with hands tied behind their backs, and they could not, even had they been willing, jockey along their mounts, and swing with the stride as the pursuers were doing.

But behind the captives was the girl with her whip. She rode like one possessed. There was a fierceness in her face that amazed Barney.

His heart rose as he glanced back at her. And each time, she had a wave of the hand and a shout for him.

The valley turned from rolling into broken ground. It narrowed to a chasm again, the walls lifting straight up, almost from the side of the water that flashed down the center of the canyon.

As they galloped, the hoofbeats ringing loudly in their ears, Barney saw that McGregor was laughing with a savage exultation. He had the meaning of that laughter explained, in another moment, for as they came toward the head of the canyon, they found that it pinched away almost to nothing. The water of the runlet streamed down from a spring on the left-hand cliff. And across the head of the gorge there was a thirty-foot gap, where a more powerful stream had cut down through the living rock. A scattering of trees grew on the brink of the chasm on either side. From beneath they heard the mournful, rolling sound of the waters.

Another sound was beating behind them, the frantic clanging of the hoofs of the horses of McGregor's men.

And McGregor exclaimed: "Now's the time when the game changes again, Dwyer! Now's the time when *I* hold the cards. You can try to make terms with me, maybe. I don't know what I'll do with you—but you're mine—you fat-faced fool! You've ridden yourself into a trap. You should have taken the right-hand turn through that gap, back there!''

Barney Dwyer, amazed, dismounted and stood helpless at the brink of the chasm, where a fallen tree stretched its naked hulk like a natural barrier put there to guard against the danger of a fall.

"We've got to hold 'em, Barney," cried the girl. "They're on us, Barney! Get your rifle—''

She showed the way.

She had the shining length of a Winchester out of one of the saddle scabbards, and as the thundering of hoofs rolled down on them, and as Barney saw the stream of the approaching men, the girl kneeled by the wall of the ravine to open fire.

He furnished himself with a gun, in turn, but it seemed a futile gesture. For there were seven of them, and every one a chosen man, or he would not have been selected by McGregor in the beginning. Seven of them, conscious of their victory, yelling like fiends as they shot down through the narrows of the ravine.

The girl fired. The seven came on, and old Doc Adler, snatching out a revolver, aimed point-blank and returned that shot.

Sue Jones dropped her rifle and sank down at the base of the cliff clutching her shoulder. Barney, standing straight—because he was too bewildered to do anything else—had let drive from his Winchester well over the heads of the charging men. But now he saw the girl drop, and still with the rifle at his shoulder, he ran forward.

Through those narrows at the head of the ravine, hardly two men could ride, side by side, and in the lead was Adler with another of the crew. Straight at them, Barney ran, firing as he came, firing blindly.

They answered, but as they answered, they were working furiously to turn their horses.

Apparently they had come charging with the certainty that the enemy was backed helplessly against a wall. And this madman, this Barney Dwyer whom they knew to be capable of strange things, was actually advancing against them on foot, his rifle spouting fire as he came.

He wanted to shoot to kill now, but there was such a red rage on him that he could not take aim. He did not need to. The big forty-five caliber slugs from the Colts were fanning wind into his face, but not a one of that seven had the coolness to pause, halt his horse, and take deliberate aim.

As though the charge of Barney had been the sweep of a river from behind a broken dam, it picked up the cavalcade and hurled it yelling in terror down the narrows of the ravine.

They fled far off. The uproar died away into a distant murmuring. And then Barney, standing still, wondered why it was that his heart was dead in him.

He remembered, then. It was the fall of the girl that he had seen. He turned toward her, hardly daring to let his eyes see the tragedy that he expected, and as he turned, he saw her ripping a fragment of white cloth into strips for a bandage. All her left arm and shoulder were crimson from the wound.

Yet she shouted, in a glory of triumphing! "Oh, Barney, you drove them like a lot of curs! God made only one like you!"

24

Yes, he had driven them like dogs. They had gone swirling back before him. They had shouted and cursed the men who blocked their way. They had gone shrinking away from him, with frightened yelling, as though every man expected bullets in his back, at once. But there was no sense of glory in Barney Dwyer.

He simply ran over to the girl and dropped his rifle on the ground. He held his hands out toward her, a little, helplessly. He could not see her very well, nothing but the white skin of her arm and shoulder, and the red of the blood running on it. The arm hung down dangling, worthless, useless.

"What have they done to you?" said Barney. "Oh, Sue, what have they done?"

"Hold the end of this—no, that other end. Wind it around under the arm. Press hard. Harder. Stop shaking, Barney!" she commanded. "No, hold this other end, and I'll do the winding! We have to hurry. We have to hurry and do something. They can climb up to the top of the cliff, and once they're on top, they'll kill you. Then everything would be finished. We've got to hurry. I'm all right. Stop shaking. I'm not going to die! Hold my arm like a vise! That's better."

He fastened his grip on that arm. All the while he stared into her face; for if he kept watching the blood, he felt that he would faint. She was sweating. Just across her forehead and her upper lip there was a sheen of sweat. But she was not pale with the pain.

"They shot you, Sue!" said Barney. "They shot at a woman. They ought to be all burned alive!"

"It was old Adler, and that doesn't count," said the girl. "He's not a man. And why shouldn't they shoot when I was ready to sift a lot of lead into them? When a woman starts shooting, she's not a woman anymore. There! Now I can navigate a little better. I've got to have it in a sling, though, I guess. Otherwise the arm will be swinging back and forth, and that will start the bleeding again."

She made the sling. The one useful hand worked with the speed and the skill of two, while Barney stood there like a lump, almost helpless.

He began to hear the great McGregor, who was in a terrible fury.

"Those are men who swore that they'd follow me to hell and back," he said. "Those are fellows who have had thousands of dollars out of me, every one of them. They've had the fat of everything. I did their thinking for them. I hung the money up in a Christmas stocking, you might say. All they had to do was to get up in the morning and rub their eyes open, and take in a few thousand dollars more! And they'd die for me. They all said that, Peary!"

"Don't talk to me," said Peary. "I don't want to hear your talk."

"Because you're sick. Because you're scared until you're sick. You and the rest. One half-wit and a scared girl—and seven men run from 'em! Only Adler had any manhood in him. I'm damned if I ever let another crook come near me. I'm through with gangs. I'll find one man, and work with him. With Adler!"

"You'll do your next work walking on air," said Len Peary.

"So will you!" exclaimed McGregor.

"I know it. I'm glad of it. I'm tired. I'm ready to quit the game!"

"Because you're yellow!" snarled McGregor.

"Maybe," said Peary. "But mostly because it's dirty. I used to think it was a sort of sport. Now I see what it really is. It's dirty! You shoot women in this game. That's how dirty it is."

The bandage was finished, and so was the sling. Sue was suffering now and she was weak. Barney could see that, by the whiteness around her mouth, and because her eyes were puckering a little in the corners, and the pupils dilating.

"Is it terrible, Sue?" he asked her.

"It's nothing. It's all right. The bandage grips a little, but that's the way it should be. Come on, Barney. We've got to hurry! Come, and we'll see what we can do."

Barney followed her to the edge of the gully. It was a straight drop of at least seventy feet to the shooting water beneath. The coolness of the running water came up damp against their faces.

"Maybe we can bridge the thing," said the girl. "Suppose that we can upend this fallen tree trunk. Then it would reach clear across to the other side. Try to upend it, Barney, will you?"

"Yes, I'll try," he said.

He put his hands on the trunk of the tree she pointed to, well down toward the narrow tip of the log. It came up with a tearing sound, it had been so soldered against the ground by the growth of fungi and weeds. It was half rotten, he saw, as he walked the trunk higher and higher into the air. The whole belly of the log was white and corrugated like cork by the damp. His hands slipped on the wet face of it.

The strain became great. Even his mighty arms could not support that weight. He had to let the log come down on his shoulder, and with great thrustings of his body he worked the burden higher and higher toward the perpendicular. The full strain of it was on him now. Every time his body shrugged at the weight, the tree waggled to the slender tip.

But the strain decreased every instant as he pushed the log up past forty-five degrees toward the perpendicular. And eventually, there it stood like a great mast.

He looked up along the flank of it, and was staggered by the knowledge that his own hands had erected that mighty shaft!

"That way—straight over to the right. Get behind it here, Barney," commanded the girl. "That's the way. Pray heaven that it will fall straight across! There—let go!"

He gave it a guiding thrust and then stepped back. The head of the tree wavered, hesitated, as a whiplash seems to hang an instant in the air before it is jerked forward and downward for the stroke. So the tree hesitated, and then whipped down.

The slender tip of it broke straight off against a tree on the opposite bank. Then the mass landed with a crash and with an ominous creaking and tearing sound inside. Plainly, the half-decayed timber was badly damaged by the fall.

"But how can we get them across?" asked Barney. "They've got their hands tied behind them. How can we get them across, or shall we leave them here?"

"We've got to put a guide rope across for them," said the girl. She had the coil of a lariat in her hand, and now she stepped out on the slender bridge.

"Sue!" cried Barney. "Come back! Don't do that! Don't!"

She was already halfway across. She could not use both hands to balance herself, of course, but she held up the weight of the lariat to secure her equilibrium a little. She stepped quickly, decisively. She came to the narrow part of the log. It gave under her, springing slowly up and down beneath her weight.

Barney dropped to his knees, and gripped the butt end of the log to steady it, a very vain and foolish effort, for she was already across and knotting the end of the rope around a small tree.

She gathered the noose end, swung it a little, and then threw it like a man throwing a lariat. Straight and true, it shot to the feet of Barney.

"Tie it to a tree!" she called in command. "It will be our guide rail, our balustrade, Barney. No, not that tree, but the one in line with—that's right!"

He made the rope tight. He pulled hard on it and turned it to a trembling cable; rapidly she came back across the narrow bridge to Barney.

"Now, then," said she, tiptoe with excitement, "you can get them over, Barney!" Take 'em one at a time, and steady 'em before you. Quick! Quick! McGregor's men may get to the top of the hill any moment!"

He took Len Peary over first, holding to the guide rope with one hand and steadying Peary with the other. It was easily done. So it was with McGregor, who cursed steadily, softly, as he stepped over the log.

Then Barney, returning, spread his hands over the face of the red mare. She began to whinny softly, as though she understood that he was about to leave her.

"Hurry, Barney!" said the girl. "You'll have her again, one day. You won't lose her."

She stepped out onto the log as she spoke, and Barney came behind her. There was no need to steady her. Her step was lighter, surer, than his own, and she kept one hand on the guide rope.

McGregor might have used these few moments to take to his heels, but he apparently realized that a man with hands tied behind his back could not go fast enough to escape from such a pursuer as Barney Dwyer. Therefore he merely stood fast by the tip of the log and glowered at the pair as they came.

They were in the very center of the log when he acted. The

tip of the fallen tree rested on a rock securely enough, but the surface of that rock was smooth, and now McGregor, with a sudden yell of savagery, thrust at the tip of the log with his foot.

It gave a foot or more, a ghastly wavering ran down the length of the tree trunk, and the girl screamed with fear.

Barney had time to hear Peary cry out and see him throw himself at McGregor. But if Peary hoped to stop Big Mack, he was much too late. At another quick thrust by McGregor, the end of the tree trunk was dislodged, and the whole length of the log hurled spearwise down into the abyss, leaving Barney hanging to the rope.

The hold of the girl was broken by the sudden loss of all footing. At the flare of her dress in the wind, as she fell, Barney caught with his left hand, and by the grace of fortune he made good his grip!

25

Another shock almost broke his own iron grip on the rope. The sudden pressure had pulled the rope down the slender trunk of the sapling to which it was fastened on the farther side of the gulf. But he maintained his hold, though his own weight and the weight of the girl depended from one hand!

Yet she seemed to be slipping away. She was a loose weight dangling there beneath him, oscillating slowly back and forth. Every instant her arms threatened to slip through the sleeves and let her fall to the white rush of water beneath them.

Vainly, Barney shouted at her. She made no answer. She had fainted!

It was a strain even for his might, but he managed to draw up her weight until he could grip a thick fold of her skirt with his teeth. Then he started to go hand over hand toward the edge of the cliff.

Still danger was not over. The devil that had inspired Big Mack before worked in him still. The rope had slid down the trunk of the sapling to the ground, and now with the razor sharp rowels of his spurs, McGregor was hacking at the rope to cut the strands.

Peary, screeching with horror, came at the bigger man like a tiger. McGregor dropped flat, let the weight of Peary tumble over him, and made him quiet by deliberately kicking him in the head.

Then he turned and struck at the rope with his spurs again.

Barney worked with a desperate speed, hand over hand. But he felt the burden slipping not from the grip of his teeth but from the dress in which it was slung like a loose and lifeless thing. Then, under the grasp of his hands, he felt the parting of a strand of the rope. It was like the bursting of a blood vessel in his brain.

But he was close, now, to the end of the peril!

His right hand reached for the rock, closed on the edge of it at the very moment that the last strand of the rope parted. And there he hung, helplessly, the girl depending from the grip of his teeth, his left hand reaching for a finger hold on the edge of the rock, when McGregor deliberately stamped on his hands!

Those hands turned numb. In an instant more, McGregor could have kicked them from their meager purchase. But now Peary, who had tried vainly twice before to check McGregor, rose from the ground and came running in again. Blood streaked the side of his face from the gash that the boot of McGregor had cut. But he came in silently, with a face convulsed. Like a charging bull, his shoulder struck McGregor.

That was the breathing space which enabled Barney to clamber over the edge of the rock and then to draw up the girl after him.

She was as limp as dead flesh. She was as white as death, too; yet she opened her eyes almost instantly. Back from the edge of the rock Barney carried her a step or two, into the shelter of the woods.

The mare was neighing desperately on the farther side of the gulch. But more important than her calling, almost more important than the returning life in the eyes of Sue Jones, was the sound of running feet that dodged away among the trees.

All the soul of Barney Dwyer yearned to be in pursuit of that fugitive. He only paused to slash the leather rein that held the hands of Leonard Peary securely lashed behind his back.

"You're free, Len!" he panted. "God bless you—you saved her. Watch over her now!"

Then he darted forward after McGregor. He heard a faint outcry behind him. It was the girl's voice, but it had no meaning to him. Nothing in the world had meaning except the pursuit of McGregor.

He leaped a fallen log, heard the crashing of a body through bushes not far away, and then all was silence before him. Had McGregor been able to hide himself?

Like an eager hound that has lost the trail Barney rushed through the bushes, turned this way and that, trampled them madly, wrenched them apart—and finally saw a fleeting shadow that slipped away without noise behind the trunk of a nearby spruce.

He had sight of the prey, and he gave tongue savegely, no words rising from his throat, only a wild cry.

He rounded the tree. The shadow flicked before him, through a screen of tall saplings.

Blindly he ran on. A low bough struck him to the ground. He rose and rushed forward through a haze of red. And then, suddenly, with a screech of terror, McGregor stood before him, his shoulders working as he strove to free his hands from the bonds.

"Not the knife, Barney! A bullet, if you want, but not the knife!"

And Barney, looking down, saw that the knife with which he had freed Peary was still in his grasp.

He used it to set free the hands of McGregor. He took McGregor by the arm. He threw away the knife. He tossed aside his Colt.

"Now there's no advantage on my side, McGregor," he

said. "I'm going to kill you, but I'm not killing a helpless man!"

He looked straight into the eyes of McGregor. He looked so deeply into them that they were like crystal wells and a white shining ghost of fear was at the bottom of the well.

"D'you call it a fair fight, when you've got the strength of a horse in your hands?" asked McGregor.

Barney caught at a low branch and ripped it from the trunk of the tree, leaving a long white gash where bark and wood stripped away with the bough. He snapped the length of it in two. He pulled away the little twigs and side-thrusting branches. It was a stout cudgel that he offered to the hand of McGregor.

"You take this. That'll make us more even," said Barney. "I don't want all the chances on my side. I wouldn't taste the killing of you, that way."

The voice of the girl came piercingly through the woods behind him. Barney stepped back half a pace.

"Begin!" he commanded huskily. "Begin, McGregor— you've got a club in your hand, now!"

The lips of McGregor grinned back from the white of his teeth. His eyes were triangles, like the eyes of a fiend.

"I'm going to smash your skull for you, Dwyer!" he said. "You've been a fool for the last time—"

He struck. He had the skill of a swordsman. The bludgeon took life in the grasp of his hand, and Barney, leaping in, barely managed to parry the stroke with an upraised arm.

The weight of the blow ground flesh against bone. Another stroke would break either arm or head. And yet he did not falter. The battle rage clothed him as if with armor. He went in swaying rapidly from side to side, somewhat like a boxer— but his hands were not closed to fists. They were open, and it was the throat of McGregor that he eyed.

McGregor struck again. A lightning flexion of Barney's body let that blow go by, and then he was in!

It was like stepping through an open door into a garden of delight. He plucked the club from the hand of McGregor as an angry man might tear a toy from the grip of an infant.

He hurled it far away. He stood close to the frantic face of McGregor. He saw the fist of McGregor shoot at him. The blow glanced from his jaw like a drop of rain. And now he laid his hands on the body of the man.

He could see two things—the body of the girl dangling beneath him, slipping through the clothes that held her limp body—and now this other thing, this white, desperate, glaring face of McGregor, who must die!

And in his hands there was the power to rend flesh like rotten cloth, to break bones like sticks of kindling.

Then another voice burst on his ear. It was not the voice of McGregor, though it was screaming. Another face came, close to his. An arm wound around his neck.

Through the thunder of his own blood in his ears, he heard his name called. It grew nearer and nearer. It was the voice of the girl, and this was she, thrusting herself between him and his prey.

"Barney!" she was screaming. "It's murder! Stop! Stop! You're killing him."

Stronger hands pulled at him. He turned his head and saw Peary, white as a ghost, trying to drag him away. He loosed the grip of one hand and with a single blow struck Peary to the ground.

He tried to refasten the hold of that hand on McGregor. Instead, his grip found the arm of the girl.

The iron and the fury went out of him, at that touch.

"You're murdering him! Barney!" she screamed again.

He stood up. His legs were so weak that they would hardly support his weight. They shook, and kept his whole body shaking.

There lay McGregor on the ground, doubled up on his side. He was limp. He looked like a dead man. Barney, was sure that it was death, indeed.

"I wanted to kill him," he said. "It wasn't murder. I gave him a club. It wasn't murder, Sue. What have I done?"

She leaned the weight of her body against him. She clung to him tightly.

"Look at McGregor, Len!" she said. "See if he's living. I can't look at his face again. Listen for his heart. He may be living!"

"What have I done?" said Barney. "He ought to die, Sue.

He tried to kill you. I thought he *had* killed you. I thought that you were going to fall!''

"He's alive," said the voice of Peary, panting heavily. "He's going to live, and I don't think his bones are broken. His legs and arms are not broken, anyway. I don't know why not! I thought iron, even, would have broken!''

"Thank God for that!" said the girl. Her strength came back into her that instant. "Sit down, Barney. Sit down here.''

"Everything was a wall of flame. I couldn't see clearly through it," muttered Barney. "Sue, have I done something terrible? Look at me. You're afraid of me! Why are you afraid of me, Sue?''

She slumped to the ground. She dropped her head against her knees and began to weep, wildly, uncontrollably.

Barney looked from her trembling head up the long, brown trunk of a pine tree to the small patch of blue sky above. Then he stared into the face of Len Peary, who kneeled beside the body of McGregor. And McGregor was beginning to move his limbs. With every move, he groaned.

"What'll I do, Len?" asked Barney. "You saved her, back there. Tell me what to do, now!''

Peary stood up. There was a great red welt across the side of his face where the hand of Barney Dwyer had struck him, not many moments before. The footsteps of Peary were unsteady as he came to them and laid his hand on the unwounded shoulder of the girl.

"Quit it, Sue," commanded Peary. "You're the only one who can handle him. What if he *did* break loose for a minute? He'd been tormented almost to death. It was enough to drive anybody crazy. Pull yourself together. Speak to him.''

She lifted her head toward Barney. There was love in her eyes, he thought, but there was fear in them also.

She said nothing. Peary leaned over her, speaking earnestly.

"If you'd been with him, it would have been all right," he said. "If you stay with him, he'll never go wild again. You've got to stay with him all your life. When a man like Barney catches fire, you can't expect to see a small flame.

He's not like the rest of us. We're second growth stuff, and he's the real forest!''

The fear went out of her eyes, little by little. "I came in time," she said, at last. "And I'm never going to be that far away from you again, Barney! Not while we both live.''

McGregor could walk, though he staggered now and then, as they started. And they went on through the end of the day until they saw the lights of Coffeeville before them. Peary left them there, for he could not venture into the reach of the law as yet.

"You've done your job with me, Barney," he said. "If ever I'm cleared in the eyes of the law, I'm going back to the ranch and work. I've learned my lesson. There's no easy money in this world!''

He left them. They went on down the pass with the lights of the town spreading out before them, to the right and to the left.

"Shall we take him in?" asked Barney. "I've stopped hating him, Sue. I hope that I'll never hate another man. Shall we take McGregor in, or give him another chance, like Len Peary's chance?''

"We have to take him in," answered the girl. "As long as there's life and freedom for him, he'll never rest till he has another chance to kill you, Barney.''

That was why they went on into the town. They could hear an uproar from a distance. Everybody was out in the streets. It was McGregor who was recognized, and the others in the light of his presence, as it were. Fifty shouting men brought Barney and his captive and the girl into the center of the main street and there at the jail they encountered Sheriff Jim Elder with a calvalcade of his riflemen, and many prisoners. Two forms leaped out into the mind of Barney—old Doc Adler, tied into a saddle, and the red mare drawn along on two lead ropes.

They heard the story later, when they were in the house of Dr. Swain. Sue Jones lay on a couch in the sitting room, freshly bandaged, her face pale but happy, and the sheriff told how the noise of gunfire had led him and his posse as with lights down that narrow ravine, and how the McGregor crew had been scooped up easily, with hardly a shot fired, except by that dangerous old wolf, Adler.

"But what I've done is nothing, Dwyer," said the sheriff. "We've been wanting McGregor and a crime to lodge against him all these years. With the end of him, we'll have peace all through this range. Now, man, tell your own story."

Barney looked toward the girl helplessly.

"I'm no good at talking," he said. "Ask her, and she'll say what needs to be said."

She merely shook her head, and smiled faintly, at the ceiling.

"Talking is no good," she said. "Not when you've known better things than words!"

Part
Three

26

Sheriff Jim Elder, from the window of the hotel, pointed out the Coffeeville jail, a little white frame building.

"We've got 'em there for the minute, Barney," he said to Dwyer, "but if you refuse to appear against 'em, we probably can't hold 'em long. Not unless I can get one of McGregor's gang to turn state's evidence against his boss."

"Suppose that I go into court and tell what I know about Adler and McGregor?" he said.

"Adler will get enough years to make it life for him; and they'll hang McGregor," said the sheriff, instantly. "And with McGregor gone, we'll have peace through the whole range."

Barney Dwyer put his hands together and twisted them so hard that his shoulder muscles leaped out and filled the slack of his blue flannel shirt as a hard wind fills a sail. There was trouble in his eyes, pain wrinkling his brow.

"I can't do it, Jim," said he. "I know they're bad ones, that pair. But if a man were hanged because of what I said in a courtroom, it would be poison to me."

The sheriff exclaimed impatiently: "What would they do to

you, if they managed to get out of jail, Barney? Tell me that?''

"They'd murder me if they could," said Barney. "I know that. I'm afraid of 'em, too. But to hang a man with the words I speak—I couldn't do it.''

The sheriff had many reasons for respecting Barney Dwyer, but now he stared with a mounting fury into that gentle, simple, troubled face. Words to voice all his anger came up into the throat of Jim Elder, but he choked them suddenly back. He turned his back sharply on big Barney Dwyer and made two rapid turns up and down the room. When he halted again in front of Barney, he snapped: "Will you talk to Sue Jones before you make up your mind?''

"I'll talk to her," agreed Dwyer. "But even Sue couldn't change my mind about this, I'm afraid. I'm going out to see her now at Dr. Swain's. The doctor says that he can cure her shoulder so that there'll hardly be a sign of a scar! Think of that!''

"Think of the beast that fired the bullet at a woman!" said the sheriff. "Think of that—and think what it will mean to the range to put Adler and McGregor either in a hemp rope or behind the bars for life! I've spent years trying to hunt them down. After all my trying, you caught McGregor. It was a great thing. That's why that crowd is hanging around the hotel to see you. It was a wonderful thing that you did, Barney. But unless you follow it up with testimony in the courtroom, what you've done is as good as nothing!''

Instead of answering directly, Barney Dwyer stepped gingerly toward the window and looked down into the street.

Men lingered on the veranda of the general merchandise store and more men were talking and laughing under the roof of the hotel porch as well. New arrivals constantly galloped up, tied their horses at the long hitching rack and, before entering the barroom or joining the others on the veranda, paused for a moment to look at the red mare, near to which none of the other animals were tethered.

"D'you mean that they've come into Coffeeville to see me?" asked Barney Dwyer, his eyes growing round.

"You and the mare, yes!" said the sheriff. "And all the

women in the town are trying to get past Mrs. Swain to have a look at Sue. Well, it's no wonder. Sue is the heroine, and you're the hero, Barney. You'll have a crowd at your heels the rest of your life, after the things you've done. And I hope the crowd bothers you as much as the flies are bothering your mare down there!''

There was a good-humored petulance in his voice as he spoke. But Barney Dwyer held up a protesting hand.

''I'm no hero, Jim,'' said he. ''I was frightened, too, a lot of times. I was terribly frightened, as a matter of fact. I—I—how can I get away from that crowd, Jim? Will you tell me? I've got to see Sue, but I can't wade through all those people and—''

He blushed; with misery in his eyes he appealed to the sheriff, but Jim Elder merely grinned.

''You've made your medicine, and you'll have to swallow it,'' said he.

''No,'' exclaimed Barney Dwyer. ''I could go down the back way!''

''What back way?'' asked the sheriff.

Barney pointed to the window at the rear of the room. Then he picked up a forty-foot rope that hung on the back of a chair, neatly coiled, and carried it to the back window. There was a long drop beneath him to the yard below, which was walled about by a high board fence. Barney tied one end of the rope firmly to a chair.

''Are you going to take the risk of breaking your neck?'' demanded Jim Elder angrily, ''for the sake of avoiding that gang, which only wants to shake hands with you and buy you drinks?''

''Whiskey makes my head buzz around and around as though there were flies inside it,'' said Barney. ''And yet if I don't take a drink men are angry. It hurts their pride. And then there's apt to be fighting, and I hate a fight, Jim! You see how it is?''

The sheriff peered at him as though he were a great distance off; he peered as a man does when the glare of the desert is hurting the eyes.

''You beat me, Barney!'' he exclaimed. ''But in the name

of God, let me try to make you see reason before you break
your back falling out of a hotel window. I'm asking you to
remember that every low trick a man can use on another man,
McGregor's tried on you. And all I'm asking of you is to take
that devil out of the world by simply standing up in a
courtroom and telling the truth as the law requires you to do.
It's not even vengeance. It's justice. It's doing your duty to
the world!"

Barney Dwyer paused to consider, with his mild eyes
contemplating his thought. Slowly his big head began to
shake from side to side in denial.

"Maybe you're right, Jim," he said at last. "You know a
lot more than I do. A whole lot more! But I'll tell you
something—once I had McGregor in my hands and I was
killing him. I was blind with the joy of killing him, till Sue
stopped me. Afterward I swore that I'd never lift a hand
against any man, except to defend myself. And I won't lift
my voice, either, Jim. Not even in a courtroom!"

The sheriff groaned, made a gesture of surrender with both
hands, and said no more. Barney Dwyer was already through
the window. He wedged the chair carefully, threw out the
length of the rope, and then went down it, hand over hand,
rapidly.

The sheriff leaned out. He saw the red bandana fluttering at
the neck of Dwyer. Near the bottom of the rope, he saw him
loose his grip and drop lightly.

He looked up and waved a cheerful hand at the sheriff,
smiling.

"He makes no more of that circus trick," grunted the
sheriff, "than I'd make of walking across the room. He's
different from the rest of us, body and brain! Plain different!"

Barney Dwyer had turned to the high board fence. He
swung himself lightly over and dropped onto the sunburned
grass of the farther side.

It was a little winding lane that led down to the side of
Coffee Creek. He glanced up and down it, and sighed as he
made sure that there was no one in sight. He was wrong. A
lad with a homemade rod in one hand and a small string of

fish in the other was drifting slowly up the slope, and seeing Barney he had paused at once to stare.

Now Barney tilted back his head and whistled three quick, sharp notes. After that he waited. The red mare would come at once, when she located the direction of the whistle.

And he waited for her with his head thrown back, smiling a little in expectation. With her speed and grace under him, he would soon be far from the annoyance of crowds.

He heard the whinny of the mare, as familiar to him as the voice of a human to another man. Then another voice shot up close by, the yell of a boy who cried: "He's here! Come quick! Barney Dwyer! Barney Dwyer!"

That voice jumped with electric tinglings along the nerves of Barney. He turned, and as he turned, he saw the boy come at him.

"Barney Dwyer! I've got Barney! He's here! Hurry up, everybody!"

The freckled face of the lad was convulsed with delight. He dodged the outstretched hands of Barney, and caught at his belt.

"Barney Dwyer!" he shrieked. "I've caught Barney! Hurry!"

With one hand, Barney lifted the wriggling youngster by the nape of the neck. The terrible grasp of the other hand he laid on the wrist of the boy, trying to pull his grip loose.

But he was afraid to use his strength. Even the iron-hard bones of grown men were apt to snap under his hold. Therefore he went gingerly about the work of detaching the grip of the boy.

And the youngster yelled louder than ever.

Here at last came the red mare, though late. And Barney could see that she limped.

He was horrified. He looked again, and he saw that an iron band had been hammered into place around her left foreleg. It jounced up and down and made her gallop shorten to a hobble. While behind her, led by her going, streamed the head of the mob, rushing straight down upon Barney Dwyer!

They all cheered tumultuously. Barney would have been glad to escape from them, but he could not manage that while the mob was shouldering about him, and the red mare was unable to run. So he leaned and laid his grasp on the round of iron that encircled her leg.

It was an ordinary horseshoe the toes of which had been hammered in to make the ring complete and enclose the slender cannon bone of the mare's near foreleg.

"Now we're gunna see!" exclaimed a big fellow with the soot of the blacksmith shop still on his forearms. "Now we're gunna see, and now we're gunna be able to tell what liars some folks is that say that they seen him *break* a horseshoe!"

Barney already had his grip inside the heavy iron ring, and he tugged at the iron circle.

The flesh of his fingers brushed against the bone vainly, until he heard the blacksmith's remark, and when he perceived that there was a silly trickery about the whole thing, and that this had been devised as a test for his strength, a fury boiled up in Barney Dwyer. He jerked. If that band were of iron, his hands and wrists became of steel and unbent it enough to draw it free from the leg entirely.

He faced the blacksmith and hurled the unbent shoe down into the dust before him. Barney Dwyer was utterly mindless of the shout of joyous astonishment, and of the long, amazed face of the blacksmith.

"It's all right to make a fool of *me*," exclaimed Barney, "but if you touch my horse again, I'll see what *your* bones are made of!"

The big blacksmith said not a word. He merely bent and picked up the unbent horseshoe from the dust at his feet and then slunk away through the crowd.

Barney swung on high into the saddle. They scattered back before him. He was about to ride off when a tall fellow with an authoritative air came out from the side of the lane, where he had been watching critically. He had just suppressed a smile of satisfaction, and now he said: "Dwyer, I'm Parmelee of the Parmelee Ranch. Will you talk business with me?"

Barney instantly jumped down to the ground. There were scores of witnesses of the conversation that followed.

"Yes, Mr. Parmelee?" said Barney.

"You know my ranch?" asked Robert Parmelee.

"No, sir," said Barney respectfully.

"It's up yonder," said Parmelee. "Up there in the pass. Up there in the hole-in-the-wall country. D'you see?"

He pointed toward the ragged, distant tide of the mountains.

"I see," said Barney.

"I need a foreman to take charge for me," said Parmelee. "Will you take the job? It's a hundred and fifty a month—to start with!"

Barney glanced hastily around him and flushed. He wished that he might be alone with Parmelee to make the confession that followed. But the truth had to out.

Then he said, confronting the lean, shrewd face of Parmelee: "The fact is that I'm not fit to boss a gang, Mr. Parmelee. I'm not a very good hand with a rope. And I don't know how to handle cattle very well. I couldn't take such a responsibility as running your ranch for you."

At this, a little hush fell over the crowd. They knew Parmelee. A good many of them had eloquent reasons for knowing him. He himself grinned sourly.

"I'll run my own ranch and handle my own cows," he said. "I have plenty of acres of grasslands. I have plenty of dirty rustlers for neighbors, too. I want punchers made of iron. I want punchers that Winchester bullets will bounce off. And I want a foreman that's able to bend those iron men. Dwyer, don't tell me whether or not you're the right man. Just tell me that you'll do your best."

"I'll do my best," said Barney, staring. He was like a child forced to answer a teacher.

"Then come up there tomorrow. I'll be waiting for you," said Parmelee.

27

It was later in that day when Harris Fielding, lawyer extraordinary, talked with his two clients in the Coffeeville jail.

Adler and McGregor stood on one side of the steel grating, and little Harris Fielding walked impatiently up and down on the outer side of it. The guard stood in a far corner, only making sure that the visitor made no effort to pass anything into the hands of the accused men. It was an old frame building, and yet it had an excellent reputation, for the cells were of the best bars of tool-proof steel, and the sheriff saw to it that the guards were of the best sort of fighting material.

Harris Fielding was terse and excited. As he walked up and down, he talked only while he was pacing in one direction. As he moved in the other, he silently fixed his glance on the long white face, the white hair, the black eyes of Doc Adler—eyes that were perennially young, for evil was in him like a bright fountain of youth. Doc Adler sat in a chair, his head thrust forward by the crook in his back, while McGregor stood beside him, resting a hand on the back of the chair. McGregor did the talking, his face hard as iron.

"I've got good news and bad news," said Harris Fielding.

"At the price we pay you, you ought to have nothing but good news," said McGregor.

"You think I can pull a man clear when he's all in hell except one fingertip?" snapped Harris Fielding, shaking a bony finger at McGregor.

"You've done it before," said McGregor. "And you can do it again. What's the good news?"

"Big Barney Dwyer refuses to press the case against you. He won't go into the courtroom and give testimony against you," said Harris Fielding.

"He thinks that he can make us forget other things he's done, eh? He's turning yellow, is he?" said McGregor.

"I'm telling you the facts, not the motives," answered Harris Fielding. "But from what the people say, there's no fear in him. Now for my bad news, and it's enough to overweigh the good news. Your man, Justis, the big fellow with the long black hair, is ready to turn state's evidence."

"Justis?" said McGregor calmly. "Then get to him, and stop him."

"I've got to him," said Harris Fielding. "I didn't need to wait for orders to do that. I got to him, but I can't stop him."

"Money will stop him. Money will choke him—the traitor!" said McGregor.

"Money won't stop him. He won't take a penny. He's sick of you, he says, ever since Adler put a bullet through the shoulder of the girl. He says that a man who would shoot a woman isn't fit for murder, even. Adler did it, though. And Adler was your right-hand man."

"I've put money by the tens of thousands in the hands of Justis," remarked McGregor, "and now he turns on me, the snake!"

"He says that you and Adler are a disgrace to the West," said Harris Fielding. "He says that burning is what you ought to have, and not hanging. He says that he'd like to light the fire that roasts you."

McGregor looked down at Adler, and Adler looked up at McGregor.

"When I'm out of this," said McGregor, "I'll call on Mr. Justis even before I call on Barney Dwyer."

"Boys," said Harris Fielding, pausing at last in his pacing and standing directly before the pair. "I don't think that you're going to get out!"

"We're going to get out. I have some things to do before I die," answered McGregor. "What's the idea, Fielding? Trying to shake us down for a bigger retainer?"

"If I can't do more than I've managed up to this point," answered Fielding, "I'll give back the retainer. I'm not trying to shake you down. I'm just telling you how near the rope you are."

"You don't see a way to save us? What about the judge? You said that you knew him!"

"I do. And he's as crooked as a dog's hind leg. But when I talked to him last night, he said that there's nothing that he dares to try when the trial takes place. He says that the whole district around here thinks that Barney Dwyer is a hero."

"Hero? He's a half-wit!" said McGregor.

"He may be a little simple about some things," answered Fielding, "but I should say that he's something more than a half-wit. At least, he's beaten you and Adler—the wisest crooks in the whole range! He's beaten you over and over."

With one voice, both Adler and McGregor croaked: "Luck! He had some crazy luck! Beginners' luck. He couldn't sit in with us through the whole game. We'd have his scalp," added McGregor.

"Maybe you would. I hear you say so," said Harris Fielding. "But just now he's riding on top. The decent men in this town won't speak to me, simply because they know that I'm your hired lawyer. No wonder the judge says that he wouldn't dare to favor you. He'd be lynched. And any juryman who failed to find you guilty would be lynched, too—and pronto! Maybe I paint a black picture for you, but it's a true one. If you stand your trial in Coffeeville, you're a pair of dead ones."

McGregor closed his eyes and grew slightly pale.

Adler remarked: "Well, now that we know the rock-bottom, we can start building."

"Building on what?" snapped McGregor.

"Building to get out of this place—this jail. If staying on here means hangin', then we gotta leave!"

"How'll you get out?" asked Harris Fielding.

"With our brains," said Adler.

"Burn your brains!" growled Fielding, and walked straight out of the jail.

He went to the hotel, packed his bag, and paid his bill.

"I wash my hands of the Adler-McGregor case," said Harris Fielding. And he went to the railroad station. Stepping out briskly in his natty suit of gray tweed. "They're as guilty as hell—and that's why I'm washing my hands of the case," said Harris Fielding, unprofessionally.

As a matter of fact, he thought that the pair were little better than dead men.

An hour later, big, long-haired Justis had sworn out the statement by which he saved his own neck. It was an economical statement. As for Adler, it could be proved that he had fired a bullet at a woman with intent to kill. That would be enough to settle him in a Western law court. As for McGregor, the statement of Justis proved very simply and with concrete evidence that it was not young Leonard Peary who had shot and killed Buddy Marsh, driver of the Coffeeville stage to Timberline. Instead, Peary was cleared of the murder and the blame was placed squarely on the shoulders of McGregor.

The district attorney was very contented after he had that statement in his hands. Coffeeville was contented, too.

But in their adjoining cells at the jail, that evening, hope was not dead in the breasts of McGregor and Adler. Like a strange harbinger of better fortune, there arrived a visitor to call upon McGregor, and he was permitted to chat with the captive for a moment, standing in front of the bars of the cell. For everyone knew that this was just old Wash, who for years had been the servant to McGregor, and before him to the honorable family from which McGregor descended.

So the jailor let in Wash, and stood only near enough to see that nothing was passed from hand to hand.

Old Wash, his head bowed, stood in the aisle in front of his master's cell and let the tears roll down his face.

Adler sat with his buzzard face pressed close against the bars, watching, listening. Like a bird, his eyes were sharp as polished beads.

But the voice of McGregor went on softly, smoothly, saying: "Wash, did you bring down the bunch of skeleton keys and pass keys?"

"Yes, sir," said Wash.

"Take those keys out to the edge of the town, up the creek, tonight, as soon as it's dark. There's a grove of poplar trees, yonder. Take the keys there. And have two good horses there. And wait."

"Yes, sir," said Wash.

"I may not come tonight, or tomorrow night. But have the keys and the horses there. Have them there every night. Every night until they hang me by the neck."

"Yes, sir," said Wash.

"Have you brought plenty of money, Wash?"

"Ten thousand dollars, sir."

"That ought to be enough. Get the finest horses that you can buy. Have rifles and revolvers. Everything that I might need. You understand?"

"Yes, sir," said Wash.

"And if I hang, Wash," went on McGregor, "all of that money is yours. That and everything else you can put your hands on. You know where to find it, too!"

"Old Wash ain't gunna need money, if you come to an end, sir," said the servant.

"Don't talk rot," said McGregor. "You'll live twenty years more. Now get out of here and do what I tell you."

So Wash left the jail, and presently afterward, the head jailor went his final rounds for the night, and lingered to shine his lantern on the manacles that bound the hands of McGregor and Adler. He nodded, satisfied, and moved on his way. The jail settled into darkness broken only by the glow of a single smoky lantern toward the center of the cell room. Other men began to snore; but Adler and McGregor were talking in small whispers, bending their minds on the problem of life or of death.

"Fielding has run out on us," said McGregor.

"It's a sinkin' ship when that rat leaves it," commented Adler.

"Burn our brains!" muttered McGregor. "He told us to burn our brains to get us out of here!"

"We'll burn 'em, then," said Adler. "There ain't a tight place in the world that thinkin' won't make wide enough for a hoss and man to ride out of safe and sound!"

"Ride us out of here, then, Doc," said McGregor.

"Burn our brains, eh?" muttered Adler. "Burn our brains!"

"There's twenty chinks and crannies right through the crazy old walls of the jail," said McGregor.

"It ain't the walls, it's the steel bars inside of 'em that count," said Adler. "It's a funny thing, Mack. Here's me, that's beat the law all of these years. I put my brains up agin some of the smartest that ever stepped. And always I beat 'em, till I come agin this Barney Dwyer!"

"The half-wit!" snarled McGregor.

"Don't talk down about him, Mack," said Adler. "Because if you make him small, you make us mighty tiny! These here mountains knew us like sheep know a pair of old bellwethers. But still he beat us both—him and him alone!"

"Luck is the difference," said McGregor.

"Burn our brains to get out—burn our brains!" murmured Adler. "And even Harris Fielding has gone and left us. He wouldn't leave while there was a ghost of a hope. That ain't his way."

"Damn him!" said McGregor. "If we could get some good saws in here————"

"There'd make a terrible screechin' on the tool-proof steel," said Adler. "And there's gents on guard here night and day, always watchin' and waitin' for a whisper out of our cells."

"We've got to think," insisted McGregor.

"Never crowd your brain, son," said Doc Adler. "Never put a whip on your brain. A gent's mind is a free worker, till it's crowded. Take when you try to remember a name that slipped your memory. You try hard. You force. And the doggone mind lays right down on you like a balky hoss, and don't do nothing. But suppose that you quit tryin', and just whistle a tune, and make yourself a cigarette, and right away that name pops up in your mind, easy as nothin' at all."

"All right," said McGregor. "But every night that passes brings us a night nearer to hell. They'll put us on trial tomorrow."

"Burn our minds, eh?" said Doc Adler. "Burn our minds to get away? No, but by God, we might burn the jail!"

"Rather die in a fire than by a rope?" asked McGregor.

"I've got the head of a match in the pocket of this coat," said Adler. "And the wood of this here wall is dry as tinder. And there's an old newspaper in my cell. By thunder, Mack, it's the right idea."

"They take us out because the damn jail begins to burn? Is that it?"

"That's it," said Adler. "Anyway, we'll see."

Presently, faint sounds of the rustling of paper came from his cell. After that, there was the crackling noise of a match being struck—a most illegal act in that tinderbox of a building. And immediately afterward, the thick, sweet smoke of burning paper poured out of the cell of Adler.

Neither he nor McGregor uttered a sound. The other prisoners slept soundly, and the guards gave no token. Into the noise of the burning of the paper came another sound, the sharp, resinous crackling as the dry pine boards that composed the wall of the jail began to catch from the heat.

The moment that they were fairly ignited, a gust of wind took the fire rushing and snapping up the outer wall of the jail. A man yelled loudly from the street. And as a gust of heat swept through the jail itself, other prisoners wakened and began to screech.

"Fire! Fire!" There was a trampling of feet. The guards came running. Water was brought. The whole floor of the jail was soon awash with it, but that did not master the flames, which were running to the apex of the roof by this time.

The jailor came and shook his fist through the bars at Adler.

"You did this, damn you. I've a mind to leave you there to roast!" he called.

But already the doors of the cells were being unlocked and the prisoners turned loose. Adler and McGregor among the rest were herded into the street in front of the flaming building.

There were twenty prisoners, most of them in for nothing more than vagrancy. And there were only four guards. They picked out the chief prisoners, however. The head jailor himself took charge of big McGregor. And his next best man was with old Doc Adler. Yet giving so little heed to his charge that he merely kept a firm grip on Adler's arm and watched the flames of the burning jail, while Doc Adler whispered to the tramps nearby: "Now, boys, one rush and we're all as free as the day we were born. All together, and one good rush, and we'll kick their coppers in the face, and slide out of Coffeeville while the rest of the town is still throwin' water to keep the whole place from burnin' up!"

From far and near, as the flame from the jail shot high in the air and great showers of sparks descended over the town, men could be seen on rooftops, little black forms against the sky, hauling up buckets of water from the ground and wetting down the shingles.

There were surprisingly few, except women and children, left to watch the conflagration.

And the little herd of prisoners, closely compacted by the guards who watched over them, began to stir a little. A muttering came up from them, just as a moaning sound will come up from a herd that is bedded down in uneasy weather.

And as a herd will start into a stampede when a single cow leaps to its feet and rushes off, so the whole gang of the prisoners got into sudden motion when a huge black in the center of the bunch bounded high into the air and yelled: "Boys, I'm goin'!"

There was one instant of wavering. Then the whole crowd lurched straight forward.

The guards were brave men and knew their business. But they were kicked to the ground, or beaten down with the blows delivered by manacled wrists, and the whole mass of the prisoners swept off up the street.

At the very next lane, two figures detached from the rest and slipped down to the edge of the creek. Stealthily they worked back up the side of the water until they came to a small grove of trees and into that they disappeared.

Behind them, the jail was already rotting to the ground in a welter of flames, leaving the red-hot skeleton of the cells still standing, unharmed.

28

To Barney, all the news of that escape was lacking. He had left Coffeeville in the afternoon, with his roll of belongings strapped behind his saddle, a Winchester thrust into the saddle holster under his knee, and a heavy Colt revolver. He merely paused at the house of Dr. Swain to see Susan Jones.

It was a hot afternoon, and the doctor and his wife had carried the girl into the shade of the house, in the garden. There she lay, propped with pillows on a small camp-cot, when Barney came to her. Mrs. Swain promptly got up from

the chair where she had been sitting to read to the girl and
offered that seat to Barney, but he could not disturb her
comfort. It hardly even occurred to him that it might be better
if he were alone with Sue Jones. He wanted to be near her, to
touch her hand, to look closely into her face, and for that
purpose, he dropped on one knee beside the cot.

The girl's face was an almost even white when he came. It
turned at once to an almost even red. She bit her lip. She was
ashamed of Barney for not having sufficient understanding to
see that they should be alone. She was ashamed of herself for
not appreciating more his calm lack of self-consciousness.

"You stay, Mrs. Swain," she said. "It's all right. Do
stay."

Mrs. Swain remained, but uneasily.

And Barney said: "You're better, Sue. Your eye is clearer."

"I'm better," said the girl.

He took her hand with a wonderful gentleness.

"There's a Mr. Robert Parmelee who offered me a place
today on his ranch, to act as foreman, at a hundred and fifty
dollars a month. I told him that I really don't know enough to
handle the cattle. He says that doesn't matter. He thinks, for
some reason, that I may be able to handle the sort of men that
he needs to have on his place. I've told him that I'd come—if
you permit it, Sue."

The girl blushed more deeply.

"If you decided to go, of course you're the master of
yourself, Barney," said she.

"But you know," said Barney, looking at her in surprise,
"that all of your ideas are sure to be better than mine. Well,
Sue, should I go or stay?"

She seemed to be more irritated than ever by this question,
and she exclaimed: "Barney, how can I tell? Do you think
that you're strong enough to handle several hundred wild
people? I've heard about the rustlers and the squatters up
there in the mountains. Everybody has! And what could you
do with them, being only one man?"

"I don't know," said Barney. "Maybe I could do nothing,
and maybe on the other hand, I could manage to help. If Mr.
Parmelee is in trouble—why shouldn't I go to work for him?

And you know, Sue, that I have to be making a little money before we can be married.''

Mrs. Swain ducked her head and frowned in order to cover her smile. But Sue Jones saw the smile, nevertheless.

''It's true,'' she said. ''And then—there's another thing. You have to be your own manager, Barney. You have to be able to make your own decisions before you can take care of a family, I suppose?''

''Do I?'' said Barney, open-eyed. ''I didn't know that. I thought that you would always make all the decisions. I thought that wives always did, in happy homes!''

The two women looked at one another and both laughed.

''You're not angry, Sue?'' he asked her.

''No,'' said the girl.

''And if I go, you'll follow me when you're well, Sue, on the way that I take?''

''Yes,'' she said, blushing hotly.

He leaned over her.

''Will you kiss me goodbye, Sue?'' said he.

She pursed her lips, silently, and so he touched them, stood up, bade Mrs. Swain goodbye, and went out to the red mare that waited at the gate. He swung into the saddle, waved his hat in a happy farewell, and was gone.

The sound of the hoofbeats still swung back to them when the doctor's wife murmured: ''Why are you ashamed, Sue? Tell me that!''

The girl closed her eyes tightly and made a gesture with the arm that was not bandaged.

''Because,'' she exclaimed, ''sometimes I think that the gossips are right, and that he has only half of his wits about him; and then at other times I feel that he's just a great, simple-hearted hero, without malice or meanness or sharpness.''

Mrs. Swain narrowed her eyes a little, and stopped smiling.

''I understand,'' she said. ''But I'll tell you something. If he's a fool, he must be a very great one, because he's done some very great things!''

The girl nodded, and sighed.

''And I've seen some of them,'' she confessed. ''I've seen him always fearless, always true. And yet, Mrs. Swain—

sometimes I wish—sometimes I wish that he were a little less good, and a little more clever!''

"Good men are always a little simple," said Mrs. Swain. "And especially good husbands!"

She said this with a great deal of emphasis, and the two women found something between them that made them smile silently at one another.

But if Barney Dwyer showed no appreciation of the shadow that had crossed the mind of the girl, he felt it all the more keenly. As he rode the red mare up through the hills toward the Parmelee ranch, he sighed more than once. He looked up with a frown of resolution toward the sky, telling himself that he must gather his strength again, and more mightily than ever, if he were to make Sue Jones really his.

He was used to pain. His very strength had made him more often cursed than blessed for the pitchforks and the spades that he broke; until, finally, he had matched that strength against McGregor and that band of cutthroats in the mountains. His reward had been fame and popularity. His greatest reward of all had been the promise of the girl to marry him. But as he dwelt on the memory of that pretty brown face, so brown that the eyes seemed doubly blue in it, he told himself over and over that she was much too good for him. He would have to labor with all his might to hold her after she had been won.

That was the reason Barney sighed as he journeyed along. And yet he was purely happy, in a sense. He was happy because he was alone with the red bay mare, and though she had no words, she supplied him with a sort of conversation by the lifting of her head, the pricking of her ears, and the very way she paused on a hilltop to look down into the hollow beneath.

As they came to the steeper inclines, he dismounted as usual, and went on foot, and he was still on foot when he came with the evening of the day to the pass; and in the darkness he reached the ranch house. It was merely a long, low shed, with a barn behind it. He pushed open the door to inquire at the house: "Is this the Parmelee place?" And there he saw a big table with six men seated at it, and one of the six was Robert Parmelee.

The rancher did not rise. He merely said: "Put your horse up, and come in for supper."

So Barney put up the horse. He found the feed box, gave the mare a feed of crushed barley, and came back to the house. The pump stood outside the building, with several wash basins of granite ware leaning against the base of it. He pumped one of those basins full, found a wedge of yellow laundry soap, and scrubbed himself thoroughly.

When he had dried his face and hands, he stood for a moment to breathe more deeply of the purity of the thin mountain air. Then he looked upward at the black outlines of the summits and finally went into the house.

There was one lamp with a round burner to give light, and it showed him a rough, tattered set of ranch hands. They sat about smoking Bull Durham tobacco wrapped in filmy tissues of wheat-straw paper. Silently they sat, staring at the remnants of soggy cold potatoes boiled in their wrappers that remained in the dish in the center of the table, and the few scraps of beefsteak that remained on a platter in the midst of a sea of white, congealed grease.

The potato dish and the platter of meat were shoved toward him. A cook came in with a plate and knife and fork and spoon and tin cup, which were rattled down in front of him, and so Barney fell to work.

He felt hard, keen eyes fastened upon him with indifference. Only Bob Parmelee seemed to be paying no attention, until, after a moment, the men began to push back their chairs.

Then Parmelee said: "Wait a minute, boys. This is your new straw boss. This is the new foreman."

"More new than foreman, he looks to me," said one of the men insolently, and stalked out of the room. The others laughed. The braying noise of their laughter grated upon the ears of Barney, and he heard the door slam behind them as they issued from the dining room into the darkness.

"Tough, eh?" said Parmelee.

Barney nodded, frowning.

"You'll have to lick 'em into shape," said Parmelee. "I told 'em that you were the new boss. I didn't tell them the name of the boss. That might make an impression, but impressions don't last long up here, the weather's too changeable. A lot too changeable. A man has to make a new reputation up here every day of his life. Understand?"

"Yes," said Barney miserably.

"These fellows are a tough lot. Nobody but tough hombres would stay for even a day up here on my ranch. There are too many bullets in the air to suit most. These fellows have nerve, and they know their business. But they don't see any reason for doing their work well when there's nothing to show for it. The cows they take care of are off under their noses, and they can't do anything about it."

Barney nodded. His heart was growing smaller and colder.

"When the morning comes," said Parmelee, "you've got to start in. You've got to show the crowd that you're the boss. After you've shown them that, you've got to start to work to get back some of the stolen cattle. A good fifty two-year-old dogies were run off today."

"Couldn't they be tracked?" asked Barney.

"They were tracked, all right. They were tracked right onto the Washburn place. Old Washburn and his boys have those dogies now, as sure as I'm alive. I know it. The boys know it. But what can we do about it?"

"Do?" said Barney, amazed. "Why, you could go and ask for them, I should think!"

Parmelee's chair screeched, as he jumped to his feet.

"*Ask* for them?" he shouted. "You think that *asking* would get them back?"

And with that, without even saying goodnight, he stalked from the room.

Barney sat gloomily over his coffee until it was cold. Then, leaving it half drunk, he got up from the table and went out to the barn. There he leaned on the manger and patted the shoulder of the red mare for a time.

He felt comforted, and went back to the house. Half of it was evidently given up to the kitchen and the dining room; the other half must be for the bunks, so he pushed open the door at the end of the house, and was promptly covered with a deluge of cold water. The bucket in which it had been balanced on top of the half-closed door crashed right over his head and fitted down on his shoulders like a man's hat on the head of a child.

And six men sat up in their bunks to shout with joy at the spectacle he presented in the light of the single lantern.

Someone turned up the light so that he could be seen the better.

That bawling laughter, those brutal faces were all familiar to him. He had always been the butt of all the practical jokes.

So he said nothing, uttered not a word of complaint, but taking the bucket from his head and shoulders, he strove to smile—a very faint appreciation of whatever humor might be concealed in this jest.

And this smiling brought only an increase in the noise! He saw Bob Parmelee laughing even more loudly than the rest; and this amazed him. In Parmelee, at least, he felt that he should have been able to find a friend.

"Straw boss, straw-hell!" said an obscure voice.

This brought noisier mirth again.

They laughed still more, in an ecstasy of derision, as they saw Barney patiently making down his bedding roll on a bunk. But he was merely saying to himself that it was an old, old story. Why had Parmelee dreamed that he, Barney Dwyer, could handle these fellows?

His wretchedness of mind, his sinking of the heart, kept him awake for a long time. He seemed, as in the old days, once more to be walled away from his fellow men.

At last he slept, and wakening in the morning, he heard the cook already calling through the half-light of the dawn: "Come and get it! Come and get it!"

He tumbled out with the rest, and went to wash, but he had to wait until the others had finished their ablutions before he could wash in turn.

When he came into the dining room, someone sang out: "Stand up, boys. Here comes the boss!"

And a roar of laughter greeted this bright sally.

He sat down.

"Ain't that your chair, Red?" asked a voice.

They roared again, and Red most of all. He was a powerful fellow in his early twenties, with a flaring shock of uncontrollable red hair, freckles across his nose, a great blunt jaw, and pale, berserker eyes that continually craved trouble.

That miserable meal ended, finally, and Barney stood up among the last. There was only Parmelee in the room, as he turned toward the door.

"One minute!" said Parmelee. "I dunno what you have up your sleeve, Dwyer. I can't imagine what! But I know that you're making a fool of yourself!"

"I don't know what to do," said Barney sadly.

"Break one of them in two! That's the thing to do," said Parmelee.

"I don't like fighting," said Barney truthfully and gently.

"You—don't like—fighting?" echoed Parmelee, raging. "And what the devil did I bring you up here for? A Sunday school teacher? A hundred and fifty dollars a month for teaching the boys hymns, perhaps? You get on the job and whip this gang into shape before night, or you're fired, Dwyer, and be damned to you!"

29

Wretchedly, Barney dragged himself out to the barn, for the body is heavy when the spirit is weak. He saddled and bridled the mare and took her out to the watering trough. He saw the keen eyes of the others fastened upon him.

"Where'd you steal that hoss, boy?" asked Red. "Or did your pa give her to you? That hoss is meant for a *man!*"

Barney swallowed the insult with a gulp.

"I only wanted to ask you men," said Barney, "if one of you would show me the way to the Washburn place. Will you?"

"If one of us would show you the way to the Washburn place," mimicked Red. "What would you do when you got there? Get a licking?"

"I want to ask them to drive back the cattle they took away yesterday," said Barney.

They stood at the heads of their horses, staring, thunderstruck. Then, led by Red, they burst into whooping peals of mirth.

"He's gunna go and *ask* the Washburns for them dogies. He's a half-wit!" shouted Red.

The stern, quick voice of Parmelee said: "Phil, show him the way to the Washburns. And stay close enough to see whether he has the nerve to ride up to the house!"

That was how Barney found himself on the way through the ragged hills of the pass until, before him, he saw a sprawling shack like that of Parmelee, only much smaller. It was a scant two miles from the ranch, tucked back in a little valley where a scrap of ploughland stood black beside a creek, and some sheep grazed behind a log fence.

At a break in the trees, Phil said: "All right—boss. There's the Washburn house. And them are the Washburns, settin' around the table, outside of the house. Lemme see you go up and brace 'em. If they don't kick you off your hoss and clean over the divide, I'll eat my hat."

Barney rode on. There were five men seated around what appeared, at a distance, to be a table with a rounded, irregular top, but coming nearer he saw that it was simply a great boulder, with jags and knobs projecting from the side, and the top spreading out like the head of a mushroom. Around the table, eating their breakfast, appeared the Washburns. The father was gray-headed and gray-bearded. Otherwise, they were hard to tell one from the other, for all were bearded, all were huge fellows in dirt-blackened patched flannel shirts. A slatternly woman went back and forth through the doorway of the house, serving her menfolk.

No one stood up when Barney came near and dismounted. But eating was suspended for an instant while bright, savage eyes glared at the stranger.

Barney saw that he had come so far out on the rim of the world that even hospitality was forgotten, here.

"Who are you?" asked the father. "There ain't any hand-outs for bums on my ranch!"

"I'm from the Parmelee place," said Barney. "It seems that Mr. Parmelee feels that some cattle—fifty of 'em—took the wrong way across the hills, and may have gone close to your place. He wants to know if you've seen them?"

Through a blank moment of silence, they stared. Then, of one mind, the five men arose from the table and faced Barney. At the door of the house, against the blackness of the interior, Barney saw the woman standing to watch, with a toothless grin.

Said the father: "If Parmelee thinks that something of his is over here on my place, what does he mean by sendin' one fat-faced fool to get it?"

Barney was stunned. He had expected discourtesy, but not this degree of it. He had hardly known what he would do when his request was refused, but he had felt that the moment would come when his back would be against the wall. For the sake of his entire future, he would have to manage something on the spur of the moment. And that spur was now entering his side.

The father walked slowly toward him. The four huge sons advanced, spreading out a little to either side. It was like the stalking of five great wolves.

"I'll tell you what I'll do," said the elder Washburn. "I'll send fifty cows to Parmelee—the damned land-grabber!—when that there rock is tore up from the ground and rolled down the hill into the creek! I'll—"

"All right," said Barney. "Let me try the rock!"

He was glad of it. No matter for the failure. If it were a problem on which he could set the strength of his hands, he felt that he would be in heaven. So he stepped past the puzzled faces of those big men and laid his grip on the lower ledge of the mushroom-shaped rock.

Then he lifted.

Such strength as his could not easily be unlocked and

bestowed like a gesture, like the breaking of a dam. Only little by little the full current of his strength began to work.

His legs were bent, his back was slightly bowed; with all the force in him he strained until more than a ton's weight of effort drove his feet down into the earth.

The Washburns had smiled; they remained to stare. They heard the creaking of mighty sinews. They saw the whole body of this stranger shuddering with his own unleashed power.

And now, with a sudden wrench, he gave the whip-snap to his labor.

With a ripping sound, with a grinding and a wrenching, the long-embedded stone heaved up from its foundations, while a yell of wonder and dismay came from the Washburns, as though something of their own flesh were being uptorn.

The great boulder staggered, leaned. Its own weight took charge of it, and toppling over, it rolled with gathering impetus down the brow of the slope, gained speed on the descent, began to leap like a drunken beast, struck a tree, shattered it with a noise like the explosion of a cannon, and then plunged into the creek.

Water leaped up fifty feet in white spray that fell again.

"It's gone!" said Mrs. Washburn, coming tottering out from the doorway of the house. "My lands, Pete—the table's gone—it's gone!"

They stood in awe, the whole family, and stared at the hole from which the great rock had been uprooted. They stared, last of all, at the face of Barney Dwyer, which was covered with a fine perspiration. Threats they would have withstood with their lifeblood. All pleas concerning justice they would have brayed down with mulish and derisive laughter. But here they saw their jest turned into a miraculous truth.

"Jumpin'—almighty—black-headed—thunder!" breathed the father of the house.

And after a long moment, Barney said: "You'll send back the steers, Mr. Washburn?"

There was a silence.

"Who are you?" asked the oldest son, in a hushed voice.

"I'm working on the Parmelee ranch," said Barney. "Mr. Parmelee asked me to come out as his foreman."

The Washburns drew together in a solid group, half of their backs turned to Barney.

But the conference lasted only a moment. He distinguished the guttural tones of the father saying: "And when I see a sign, I reckon I know it!"

Then the group quietly dissolved and faced him.

Said the elder Washburn: "I know there was some strange cattle come over onto my range. Might be that they're the Parmelee steers. Might be that they're up yonder now. My boys'll go and take a look at the brands—and if they are—I'm gunna have them drove right over onto the Parmelee place."

"Thank you," said Barney. "That's neighborly. Mr. Parmelee will appreciate it a lot, I'm sure. Good morning!"

He swung into the saddle on the red mare. Silence followed him. Slowly he walked her back across the open ground, very slowly. But presently he heard a crashing of brush, a clacking of hoofs, and looking back, he saw a herd of young steers break out of the woods behind the Washburn house with three of the Washburn boys on mustangs driving the cattle at full speed straight toward the Parmelee ranch at the foot of the valley!

Barney came up with Phil. That worthy cowpuncher was transformed into a staring ghost who looked beyond the new foreman at the miracle of the fifty young steers that were running behind him.

At the verge of the Parmelee lands, the Washburn boys no longer rode behind the cattle, but let them scatter, and Phil skillfully picked them up and drove them well-bunched before him, as only a good cowman can, straight up toward the Parmelee ranch house.

Red and Boston Charlie were building a fence behind the barn under the immediate eye of Parmelee himself, when Barney came up. He had cantered the red mare well ahead of the returning steers, and as he approached the barn, first Parmelee and then the two cowpunchers were struck dumb.

Barney reined the mare close by.

"Where would you like to have those steers herded?" he asked of Parmelee.

The rancher stared with a hungry eye.

"How many are there?" he asked.

"I don't know," said Barney. "I just asked for as many of them as might be on the Washburn land. It didn't occur to me to count them."

"There's fifty of them, all right," said Red.

His voice was husky. His eyes seemed to have grown larger, his head smaller, his neck longer, as he stared at the approaching herd and then at the new foreman.

"By God!" broke out Parmelee, "I don't know how you've managed that, but I'll tell you one thing—it's the prettiest picture that I ever saw in all of my days! How did you get those cows back, anyway?"

"Why, I just asked for them," said Barney. "And then the Washburn boys—three of them—drove the steers back to the edge of the ranch, and Phil brought them in, as you see. Where do you want them driven, Mr. Parmelee?"

"Mr. Parmelee," said Bob Parmelee, "wants them left near the ranch house, for a while. He wants them where he can see them for a few days. You go and put your horse up and go to the house. I'll be in there to talk to you, in a minute."

Barney winced a little. The strength of Parmelee's tone seemed to threaten hard times ahead of him. Was it to be immediate discharge? Slowly he turned the mare and loped her toward the barn, while the three men he had just left eyed one another grimly.

"You started to make a fool of him, Red," said Boston Charlie.

"He seemed to me like a half-wit and a coward," said Red. "And he looked scared just now, Parmelee, when you told him to put up his hoss and go to the barn. I dunno what happened at the Washburn place. There's Phil. Call him over."

Phil needed no calling. He came up at a gallop. He dismounted with the face of one who has seen a miracle.

"All I know is this," said Phil in a low voice. "I stopped

at the edge of the trees, in view of the house. The Washburns was all there. The new boss, he rides up. The five Washburns get up and walk at him. I think that they're gunna knock him on his ear. Then a funny thing happens. You know that big rock in front of the Washburn house? Well, the foreman, he just sashays up to that rock and he tears it out of the ground————"

"Hold on!" said Red. "I've been and seen that rock, and I've handled it! What're you talkin' about tearin' it up?"

"I tell you what I seen with my own eyes, and no liquor aboard me, neither," said Phil. "He done that thing. He tore that rock up, and he threw it down the hill. I looked to see the Washburn gang turn the boss into a regular colander with their guns, but they didn't do nothin'. And pretty soon three of 'em goes up into the woods behind the house, and they come out agin drivin' the cows before 'em, and they keep right on drivin', until those steers are safe on our land, and I pick 'em up!"

Stunned bewilderment greeted this statement.

"What did the foreman say?" asked Red, actually so pale that the freckles stood forth darkly on his face.

"Nothing," said Phil, his voice more subdued than ever. "He acted like it wasn't nothing much that he had done. He come back talkin' more to his red mare than to me. And I know that what I'm tellin' you was what happened before my eyes—unless I was hypnotized, or something."

No one answered him for an instant, and then Parmelee said: "Well, I had a kind of a hope that something like this might happen. I saw a sort of a dream of it in the back of my head. But I still can't believe that it's true."

They saw Barney go in toward the house. Then a horseman rocked over the top of the nearest hill, and came swinging down toward them, a fine rider on a fine chestnut horse. He drew rein nearby and waved his hand.

"It's Leonard Peary!" exclaimed Red. "It's him that used to run with the McGregor gang, till they were broke up by that fellow Barney Dwyer. What's he want up here?"

"Hello, fellows," said Peary. "Hello, Red. Long time no see. I want to know if Barney Dwyer is up here?"

"Dwyer?" shouted Red. "What would he be doing up here? Dwyer?"

"He left Coffeeville to come up here the other day," said Peary. "And I've got news for him."

"Yes," said Parmelee. "He's here."

A sudden shout from Red and from Boston Charlie. "Dwyer?" they cried.

Then Red added: "Is that new boss really Barney Dwyer? The red mare—my God, I might of known that. I might of known him by his mare. Only, I thought that he'd be bigger. Parmelee, why didn't you tell us? Did you want him to break all our backs?"

"I wanted to wait and see. That's all," answered Parmelee. "I wanted to see how much man he'd show without an introduction. The *Washburns* seem to think that he's man enough, at any rate."

He left the two to their fence-building and went to Peary.

"Come over to the house," he said. "I'll take you to Dwyer. But look here, Peary, if you try to get him away from me, you'll have to talk big money to him! And you'll have trouble with me."

"I don't mind who I have trouble with, except with Dwyer," said Peary calmly. "But you can hear the news that I have for him."

He dismounted in front of the ranch house, and there they found Barney Dwyer sitting on the porch and whittling a stick. He jumped up at the sight of Peary, who went toward him with an outstretched hand.

"Barney," he said, "can you let bygones be bygones?"

Barney took the hand at once, very cheerfully.

"Why," he said, "I never wanted to be anything but a friend to you, Len! Is there any news?"

"There's the blackest news that you ever heard," said Peary. "Adler set fire to the jail. When the prisoners were taken out, Adler and McGregor got away! They may be up here already. And they may be picking up a gang to make trouble for you before they arrive. I came on as fast as I could to give you the word. I'm going to stick with you till this trouble is over, if you'll have me!"

"Adler and McGregor!" exclaimed Parmelee. "The devil and the devil's grandfather! Both of 'em loose?"

"Both loose," said Peary grimly. "Maybe you won't want Barney Dwyer so badly now. Because wherever he is, the lightning is pretty sure to strike before long!"

"Did you see Sue?" asked Barney.

"I saw her. She begged me to come on here and see the thing through with you."

"Is she safe?" asked Barney. "Is anything likely to happen to her?"

"Not if the whole town of Coffeeville can keep trouble away from her," answered Leonard Peary. "The men down there are watching the girl now like a diamond that might be stolen. No one can bother her, Barney, if all the guns in Coffeeville can keep danger away from her."

"Then I can stay up here," said Barney. "That is, if you still want me, Mr. Parmelee."

"Want you?" exclaimed Parmelee. "After you've brought back that whole herd of steers, without one missing? Want you?"

"There's McGregor and the gang he's sure to get together," said Barney. "He'd poison the air of the whole mountains if he could get rid of me. He'd blow up the whole ranch for you, and never stop to think twice. You understand that?"

"Yes," said Parmelee. "And he'll *have* to blow up the entire ranch to get at you. I'll tell you what, Dwyer—we've given you a pretty rough reception up here. But now we're going to show you what we're made of. My men are a hard lot. But they're men. They wouldn't be here, if they weren't. And by the Lord, Barney Dwyer, we're going to stand by you, shoulder to shoulder, if McGregor, and a thousand devils along with him, try to get at you."

30

Events thickened like rain around the Parmelee ranch that day.

Late in the morning, the father of the Washburn family rode onto the ranch and found Bob Parmelee working at accounts in the house. Old Washburn would not come inside. He sat on his mustang outside with a rifle balanced across the horn of his saddle and waited for Parmelee to come out. So Parmelee came, and a gun with him.

Said Washburn: "Parmelee, we ain't been friends."

"I'm never friends with cattle thieves," said Parmelee, calmly, watchfully.

"That's a big word and a lot of it," said Washburn. "But I'm here to say that maybe you're gunna change your mind. You got a new man on this ranch of yours, and maybe he's gunna make a whole new outfit. I've come over to talk about him."

"The new foreman?"

"Yes. That's him. He's a whole hoss boiled down to the size of a man. Now, Parmelee, me and my family, we've made trouble for you. I ain't denying it. But right from now on, all trouble stops. I ain't a gent that sees many signs, but when I see 'em, I know what they mean. I seen a sign this morning bright and early. I'm gunna pay a heed to it, too. Parmelee, what my tribe aims at from now on is friendship. If they's any cattle run off of your place, the last place that you need to look is on my land."

"I'll believe you, Washburn," said the rancher.

"Times has changed, and we've gone and changed with the times. That's all I wanted to tell you, Parmelee. So long!"

He snapped his horse about with a slap of reins, and loped the cow pony across the hills, and Parmelee, staring after him, saw that the end of his long war seemed to be at hand—if only he could keep Barney Dwyer with him!

It was not until supper time that Parmelee made his next effort. He waited until the men were seated, Peary at the side of Dwyer, and the other ranch hands watching Barney as mice might watch a cat.

Then Parmelee said: "Boys, I guess you all know the name of our new foreman. Last night, you were trying to find out. You tried hard. You tried all the time. I think Barney has

forgotten what happened last night—and part of this morning.
I don't think he bears any malice because of a few practical
jokes. Do you, Barney?''

Barney started as from a dream, and blushed a little. He
was surprised, it seemed, to find himself the center of
attention.

"No, no!" he said. "No malice. A few practical jokes—
that's all right. No malice to a soul.''

Red, hearing this, snapped up his head and looked straight
at Barney, and Barney Dwyer smiled a little, and nodded back
at him with recognition. Red slumped down a little in his
chair with a vast sigh of relief. He would not have gambled
on a six months' future for himself ten minutes before. Now
life was given to him; it was like a new birth.

Parmelee went on: "I think you boys know the other news,
too. The worst thugs on the entire range, old Adler and
McGregor, are loose again, and they're sure to come on
Barney's trail. Well, boys, that trail has come to a full stop
here. Barney Dwyer is here to stay with us for a while. I
think he's broken the back of our cattle war on his first day.
And if that's true, it will be a good place for you fellows to
work. You'll have a chance at more pay in dollars and less in
bullets. But before any of us may have a chance at the good
things that lie ahead, we've got to make Barney safe here
with us. Adler and McGregor are probably near us now. They
may be outside the black of those windows this minute,
aiming guns at Dwyer!''

There was a general start, a loud squeaking and scraping of
chairs as heavy bodies moved suddenly in them.

It was Red who stood up from the table first. He said: "I
made the most trouble for you last night, Barney. Wonder you
didn't take and bust me in two. And I'm gunna have the first
watch on you. I'm gunna go out and walk the rounds of the
house. Keep a scrap of meat and some coffee for me, boys!
I'll see that this here supper is quiet enough!''

He went to the wall, picked his gun belt from a peg,
buckled it around his hips, settled his hat over his ears, and
went straightway out into the darkness.

The others settled down. They felt not a depression but a

strength of determination and resource, such as always comes to men who have just banded themselves together. A new friendliness filled them. They looked upon one another with different eyes. Each man appeared to his companions stronger; more valiant, more dependable than ever before.

Barney, staring about him, wondered how even the strength of McGregor could break through such a force as this!

He forgot, for the instant, that there is something greater than the prowess of numbers, and that is the weight of brains, and the strength of evil, which has an edge like a poisoned knife.

At this moment there came a loud hail from outside the house. It was the lifted voice of Red. Presently he threw open the door of the house and called out: "Here's a fellow that calls himself Terry Loftus. Says that he's got a message for you, Dwyer. Have a look at him."

It was a man with a face both fat and firm who stepped through the open door and frowned at the light for an instant. He was not tall. He had a big round body and a small round face. If he smiled, it was only a stretching of his lips, and a dimple appeared in either cheek.

He came slowly forward, saying: "Which of you is Dwyer?"

"I am," answered Barney.

He stood up and went a step toward Terry Loftus.

"I'm from Coffeeville, and I've got some bad news for you, Dwyer, I've got to tell you—I've got to tell you—"

His bright, black eyes wandered for an instant. Then he fished out an envelope.

"Well, you better read this, first," he said. "Then I'll tell you the rest."

Barney Dwyer opened the letter, which was not addressed, and inside he found a sheet of paper in which a few words were scribbled in the handwriting of Sue Jones. The writing was firm enough in the beginning, but it trailed away to illegibility toward the end. And there was no signature.

He read:

Dear Barney,
Blood poisoning has started, they say. And I feel

pretty sick. The doctor says it's dangerous. A man is bringing you this letter because it seems that I ought to say goodbye if it takes you too long to—

What followed—half a dozen words—was in a scrawl that he could not make out at all.

The paper fluttered from his hand to the floor. Leonard Peary picked it up and stared. Then he groaned.

Barney was saying: "How was she when you left her?"

"Kind of delirious," said Terry Loftus. "Dr. Swain, he says that he's afraid. He wants you back there, Dwyer. They asked me to bring you word because I got a fast hoss, and I know the way."

"I'm going!" said Barney. "I'll go back as fast as the red mare can take me—"

He ran for the door and disappeared into the night. Terry Loftus followed him, and so did Leonard Peary.

There were no farewells.

But presently, as the men stood about in the dining room, muttering to one another, Red spoke up.

"Any of you ever see that fellow Terry Loftus before?"

A rattling of hoofbeats began near the barn and faded down the pass.

"Did *you* ever see him before, Red?" asked Parmelee.

"I'm trying to think," said Red. "Seems like I can remember his face all right, but I can't spot where I seen it. And I can't spot his name."

Phil broke in: "Did the sight of him make you feel good or bad?"

"Mighty bad," said Red.

"Then he's tucked away for a bad hombre somewhere inside of your head," said Phil.

Red began to stride up and down the room, his head bent, and his brow contorted.

"Now I've got it. A bar—and a hard-boiled shack up from the railroad and having some beer—and me in a corner and a few more strung along the bar, and then this here fat-faced fellow steps into the picture. He and the shack have a brawl. The fat boy pulls a gun quicker'n a wink and lets the shack have it. The shack meant a fist fight, but the fat boy, he meant murder, and that's what he done. Right through the center of the forehead he drilled that shack and dropped him dead. And the fat boy backed out through the swinging doors. Nobody moved. 'Why don't we go after that killer?' I asked. 'What for?' says the bartender. Wait a minute. I'm remembering the names he used. 'What for,' says the bartender, 'that's Dick Whalen, and he's one of McGregor's men! Want to have McGregor on your back?' ''

As Red ended, Parmelee·exclaimed: ''Boys, if this fellow is packing a wrong name; if he worked for McGregor once; then he's here to make trouble. He's got Barney Dwyer away from us. I say, we all follow on and try to find out if anything happens on this trail, tonight! Will you ride with me?''

There was only one voice, and it came from the throat of every man present, and instantly they made a rush for the door of the dining room.

31

Barney was galloping far off through the night by this time, with Leonard Peary on his left and the so-called Terry Loftus on his right. When he looked up, the long gallop of the mare made the stars seem to waver in the sky, and out of the night before him, the shapes of hills loomed faintly and were gone, and trees stood up in strange attitudes and vanished to the rear. Sometimes Loftus spoke to him, sometimes Peary; he answered them in words that had no meaning to him. For all that was really in his mind was the girl.

He had suffered much pain, but he never had suffered such pain as this. He had been in terrible danger, and tried to pray, but no prayer had come to his mute lips. But now he prayed that she might endure until he came to the house, and that she might know him, give him some message before the end.

That message would be for Barney Dywer the only important reason for a continued existence in this world.

Those were his thoughts when they came to a place where the valley pinched out to a narrow ravine in which rocks and shrubs crowded the trail on either side.

Suddenly the red mare halted. The violence of her stopping almost threw Barney from the saddle.

He urged her forward, as the others drew rein ahead of him to see what was happening. But in spite of her urging, she would not go on. She merely reared and balked and backed up instead of advancing.

"What's wrong?" asked Terry Loftus smoothly.

"I don't know," said Barney. "She doesn't want to go ahead."

"She smells trouble, then," suggested Peary. "She never acts like a fool, ordinarily. There must be something ahead, Barney. You've told me more than once that she has her reasons."

"What could be ahead?" asked Barney. "She must go on. Go ahead, girl. Get on!"

He slapped her shoulder. The mare merely wheeled in a circle and stood fast, head down, balking resolutely.

"Can't you get your hoss on?" demanded Terry Loftus with heat. "Down there in Coffeeville, there's Sue Jones with the life burnin' out of her and———"

Barney groaned. He called out loudly, and suddenly the mare bolted ahead, snorting, shying at the shadows. She swept by Loftus and Peary and was going hard when something hissed in the air above Barney's head, and then he felt the grip of a rope noose that bound his arms against his sides and wrenched him out of the saddle.

He landed with a crash in the midst of a bush. Behind him, he heard the yell of Peary and the barking of a gun. But as he stood up, he saw that Peary's horse, too, had an empty saddle.

Men rushed in on either side. They spun the lariat around him, until he was fast imprisoned. And he heard the voice of Doc Adler saying: "Good work, Terry Loftus. Brains. That's what you got. Brains!"

Then McGregor came and stood by him. He said nothing, simply devouring his prisoner in silent glance.

Then, as he turned away, other men threw Barney like a sack of bran over the saddle on the back of the mare, and they were led off.

Barney had uttered no complaint. When he considered the profound depth of the hatred of McGregor, such a thing as speech between them became a folly. It was Peary who cried out, cursing Terry Loftus.

They left the trail well behind them, turned through a wilderness of rocks and trees, and so came close to the sound of running water.

They entered a little cove, a pleasant green place with a smooth floor and a hedging of bushes and trees about it, and the rushing of water at its side, with a little lean-to built near the edge of the creek. The noise of the water was like the noise of the wind by the sea.

Into the lean-to they took Barney and Peary and flung them down on the floor. A lantern was found and lighted. The illumination showed a tumbledown wreck of a place, and yet there was a lantern and oil in the shed! Barney was able to wonder at that. He could forget fear, almost, and watch the faces of the brutal men around him, and see their grinning eyes.

McGregor had Adler and five other men with him. They were like wolves, and as wolves do, so they hunted in packs.

McGregor said: "You fellows scatter. I want to be alone here with Adler and these two friends of mine. Get out of here and put yourselves where you can be on the watch."

After the men left, McGregor took the lantern and shone its light into the face of Barney.

"Turn pale, damn you!" he said.

Barney looked straight at the light, not at the man who held it. He studied the crookedness of the wick, and the crooked flame that rose from it. He was not thinking. He was simply seeing.

"Look at him!" said McGregor.

Old Doc Adler came, like a humpbacked buzzard, and sat on his heels and stared into Barney's face.

"His eyes, they ain't changed, none," said Adler.

"I'll change 'em before I'm through," said McGregor.

"You take pale blue eyes like them," said Adler, "and sometimes they don't change none. Not even when they die. They're like steel in the color of them, and they're strong as steel, too. Maybe they won't change none."

"Damn you!" breathed McGregor, and kicked Barney in the face.

The toe of the boot landed fairly on the jaw of Barney. It struck red sparks from his brain. That was all. He was not surprised or appalled. This was nothing, compared with his expectations. They would tear him to pieces, the pair of them. They would shred him small.

It was Peary who cried out, when he saw that brutal indignity offered to his friend.

"Stop it!" shouted Peary. "You rotten pair of coyotes!"

McGregor poised a quirt, but delayed the blow.

"I don't know," said McGregor. "We don't want to waste much time on this one."

Adler went to Peary and sat on his heels again until his face was level with that of Peary, who was propped against the wall.

"Well," said Adler, "suit yourself. This here is a different sort of a gent. He'd break down. He ain't got the nerve that lasted. This here Dwyer, he's got the nerve of a bulldog. The more you beat him, the harder he'd hang on. But Peary, he's just a flash. He's a wildcat. He's good for one spring, and then he's through."

"Is he?" asked McGregor, carelessly still. "Well, I don't want to waste time on him. He's a dirty traitor. That's all. And he's going to get what comes to traitors. He's not on my mind. Dwyer is the one we've been thinking about. Eh, Doc?"

"Yeah. We been thinking a little about Barney Dwyer," agreed Doc Adler.

He stood up and turned toward Barney, and licked his gray, dry lips.

"Peary!" called out McGregor.

"Well?" said Leonard Peary calmly enough.

"You know what I do to traitors, Peary?"

"You shoot 'em," said Peary.

"And I'm going to shoot you!"

Peary nodded.

"Unwind that rope from his legs. Let him stand up," said McGregor.

"Why?" asked Adler. "Shoot him the way he is."

"I want to see him drop, when I shoot," said McGregor.

"That's the trouble with you Scotch gents," said Adler. "You got a lot of sentimentality in you, that's what you got. This here Peary dead, is what you want. Ain't that enough? You got to see him drop, too? Well, well, well! Have it your own way."

He was unwrapping the legs of Peary as he spoke.

"Stand up!" he said.

Peary had been half-numbed, so that he could not move quickly. Adler turned his foot and drove the long rowels of his spur into Peary's side.

"Up, old hoss!" said Adler, and laughed.

Peary rose to his feet. Barney, sickened, closed his eyes.

"Look!" said the voice of McGregor. "Look, Doc. That's what he can't stand!"

"Yeah," said Adler. "His nerves they run right out into the body of this here Peary, maybe. Well, well, well!"

He chuckled again.

"Peary," said McGregor, "you're going to die—now!"

"I'm better dead than one of your gang," said Peary.

"He's turning good," said McGregor. "Listen to him, Adler. He's one of those that get religion before they're hanged. They repent when they've got a rope around their necks!"

"Yeah, and I've seen and heard 'em do it, and it's a funny thing, all right," commented Adler.

He shook his head in the wonder of it.

"I'd give you some special attention," said McGregor, "instead of bumping you off like this. I'd set you to screaming until the boys who are waiting out there would take a warning and a lesson by what they heard. There'll be no more traitors in my gang, for a while."

Peary was stone-white. Barney could see that clearly, and yet, like a stone, Len Peary was steady.

"Your gang is about finished, Mack," said Peary.

"Finished, eh? What makes you think that?"

"You used to be a great man, Mack," said Peary. "But you're a great man no longer. There was a time when men used to think that you couldn't be beaten. That's what I felt about you. I knew you were a robber, but I thought, as a kid, that you were not exactly bad. You were a Robin Hood, in my eyes. Not bad, but simply strong. That's why I joined you. But you're not a Robin Hood anymore. You're just a plain robber and murderer. Barney Dwyer opened the windows and let in the light on you, and the whole world knows about you, now. The ranch boys don't talk about you. They have a new hero. They have a real hero. And that's Barney Dwyer!"

"Are you through?" asked McGregor, in a terrible voice.

"I could make a pretty long speech," said Peary. "But I've said enough to let you know why I'd rather die right here and now than be free and live to work with you again."

"Die, and be damned, then," said McGregor, gasping out the words through his teeth.

He jerked a gun out and fired—one smooth, blindingly fast movement.

It was to Barney as though he had seen lightning strike. Poor Leonard Peary dropped on his face and lay still. "Try Peary," said McGregor. "See if he's really dead."

Adler stalked to the fallen body, took Peary by the hair, and lifted the head. The mouth gaped open loosely, the eyes were open too, mere slits as dull as the dead eyes of a fish. Adler dropped the head. It bounced a trifle on the floor.

"He's dead," said Adler.

"Listen to his heart," said McGregor.

"Did you see the hole in the middle of his forehead?" asked Adler.

"Oh, is that it?" said McGregor.

"When I was your age," said Adler frowning, "I knowed where I was shootin'. I didn't have to go and look. I *knowed* where the bullet went. It was my business to know."

"You and your ages be damned," said McGregor. "Here's our main job, Doc. We've brushed the small things out of the way, and now we can give a little attention to Mr. Barney Dwyer, the hero!"

"We can give him some attention," said Adler, nodding.

"I've got some ideas borrowed from Indians," said McGregor.

"Don't go and be backward, like that," urged Adler. "This here world keeps on progressin'. I could show you some things that'd warm up your heart for you, Mack!"

"I'll bet you could, Doc," said McGregor, highly pleased. "And I'm willing to learn. Go right ahead and use that brain of yours."

"It ain't a thing to hurry with," said Doc Adler.

There was a broken-down chair in the room. He pulled this out to the center of the floor and sat down in it, facing Barney, studying him like a problem in geometry.

"You've done us a lot of harm, Barney," said Doc Adler, sadly shaking his head.

"Yes," said the gentle voice of Barney. "I believe that I *have* done you a lot of harm."

"He sounds sorry for it," said Adler, interested.

"Damn him!" said McGregor. "You'll have to hurry with your ideas a little, Doc. When I think what he's done, I want to get my hands on him!"

"And hands ain't a bad idea, neither," said Doc Adler. "Maybe handwork is the best way to finish him, but I ain't so sure. I wanta think things out. The fact is, you done us a lot of harm, Barney. Here's Mack, now, that was the kingpin in these here mountains. He was pointed to by the crooks as the king of them all. He was pointed by the honest men as a gent that had covered up his trail so well that he'd never been even once in jail! And now look at him! Look at him!"

"Shut up! That's enough!" snapped McGregor.

"Well," said Doc Adler. "Maybe it *is* enough, because you've started downhill, Mack, and from now on, you're gunna go to hell fast. Year or two, it wouldn't surprise me if you was washin' dishes for a Chink cook and eatin' the scraps off of plates for your food!"

McGregor made a nervous gesture and said nothing. Adler grinned at him, but then went on: "As for me, there was old Doc Adler that had retired. And nobody had nothin' on *him*, neither. Not until he throwed in with McGregor to put down Barney Dwyer. And then everything went wrong, and poor old Doc Adler, he's gotta put a bullet through his head, rather than be caught by the police. Because they'd jail him for the rest of his days because of the mess he's got into in his old days! And that's all because of you, Barney Dwyer!"

"I'm afraid it is," said Barney, sighing a little.

McGregor burst out: "Do something, Doc, before I throttle him—the damned half-wit!"

"Well," said Adler, "*he's* the one that could do a good, quick job of throttling, when you come to that! He's got the hands for it. He could squash out the life with one grip of them terrible hands of his. Which makes me think—suppose that we was to start with his right hand, so long as we don't think of nothin' better."

"How do you mean?" asked McGregor.

"Kill his right hand for him, while the rest of him is still alive."

"I don't follow that."

"Suppose that we wrap his right hand in a bit of cloth and soak that there cloth in some kerosene. And then touch a match to it. That would burn the flesh off his bones, and we could set and study. And by the light of that there burnin' hand, Mack, we might see our way clear through to something worthwhile."

McGregor strained his head suddenly back and stared up at the ceiling.

"Ah, Doc," said he. "I was wondering if it were worthwhile to wait, like this. But now I see that it *is* right. You've found one perfect thing to do. We'll think of other things, for other parts of him. Unfasten that right hand—but treat it like dynamite!"

That, in fact, was what they did. They held a gun at the head of Barney while they freed his right forearm from the ropes. McGregor then ripped the shirt from the back of the prostrate body of Peary, and that cloth was tightly wrapped around the hand of Dwyer and soaked with kerosene from the lantern.

Doc Adler sat on his heels and looked into the eyes of Dwyer.

"They ain't changed. His eyes ain't changed, Mack," he announced regretfully. "Seems like he's quite a man, Mack! How come, Barney? What holds you together? If you ain't sad about yourself, what about that pretty gal, that loves you so much?"

"I never was worthy of her," said Barney.

32

"Scratch a match, Mack," said Adler.

It was done. McGregor, smiling with a terrible and hungry joy, held the match to wait for final instructions from Adler, who seemed such a master hand at this business.

"We touch this here match to the rag," said Adler, "and that's the end of your right hand, Barney. A doggone famous right hand it is, too. There ain't a man in the mountains that would dare to stand up to that hand, nor no two men, neither. And now it's gonna go up in smoke, and who'll make up the difference to you, Barney?"

"Ay," said McGregor, "what is there that can make up *that* difference?"

"There is God," said Barney slowly.

"By the jumping thunder, he's got religion!" exclaimed Adler. "And that spoils everything!"

"Damn him!" said McGregor, as the match went out against the tender tips of his fingers. "I knew that he'd sink a knife in us, some way."

"It's religion that does it, Mack," commented Adler. "You find it where you don't expect it, and you can't never beat it, I've noticed. It's a funny thing that you can't never beat it.''

Rapid footfalls swept toward them.

"Mack!" called a voice.

McGregor hurried to the door of the shed.

Barney, looking vaguely before him, saw something move on the floor. It was the hand of Peary! It contracted slowly and opened again!

And a golden bolt of hope darted through Barney Dwyer. The life of Peary might endure, after all!

"There's half a dozen men up on the trail," said a voice in the outer darkness.

"Half a dozen? What about 'em? Let 'em go!" said McGregor.

"Maybe they ain't inclined to go," said the other. "They're flashin' lights on the trail and studyin' signs. Might be that they're lookin' for us, eh?"

"If they're looking for us—we'll blow them to hell. I won't have this job spoiled in the middle."

He added: "Go back up to the trail, and watch with the rest of 'em. I'm following on."

The footsteps retreated. McGregor turned back into the room.

"Tie that hand against his body again, Doc," he commanded. "We'll go up there and see what's what."

"Suppose we come back and find this gent gone?" complained Adler, busily obeying instructions, nonetheless.

"He might roll as far as the door—that's all," said McGregor. "Don't be a fool."

"I don't like it," answered Doc Adler. "There's a pricklin' up my spine that makes me not like it. But—you're the boss, Mack."

So the right forearm of Barney was once again gathered in the invincible strength of the ropes against his body, and McGregor left the place. At the door, he paused to strike at the head of the red mare. Then he ran on.

"Hey, Len!" called Barney cautiously.

He received no answer. He rolled himself across the floor to his friend, and called at his ear: "Peary!"

A faint groan answered him.

"Peary, can you wake up—can you cut the ropes on me?" pleaded Barney.

A faint sigh answered him, and he knew that there was no hope of rousing the unconscious body of Peary to give him a single stroke of help.

They would be back before long, he could be sure.

Barney looked around for help. So much as a sharp-edged nail might be enough, projecting from the wall, for him to chafe through a few strands of the rope until he could snap it with a great effort of his arms.

But there was not a sign of anything that faintly resembled a tool. Nothing was near him on which he could look with pleasure, except the bright eyes of the red mare, in the doorway.

He rolled toward her, never thinking of what he could manage when he reached her, and as he floundered forward, she actually stepped through the doorway, and stood there whinnying a little, her knees bent with terror at finding herself inside this enclosure with the smell of blood in the air, but drawn by the sight of her master wallowing toward her like some strange animal!

Barney heaved himself to a half-erect sitting position. It was the limit of his ability to move. If once he could reach that saddle, he could guide her by word of mouth wherever he pleased. But he might as well have hoped to leap on the back of an eagle!

She stamped on the floor. A cloud of dust rose into his face, and the stirrups flopped just above his head.

That was what gave him the idea. He caught the leather edge of the stirrup in his teeth and hissed softly at her.

The red mare whirled and bounded out of that place of doom like a thunderbolt, almost wrenching the teeth from Barney's head, and leaving him behind!

When he recovered from the shock, he worked his way snakelike through the doorway into the open. His voice called her back, still trembling and uneasy. And again she snuffed at him, and again the whinny came from her throat as softly as a human voice.

He gained the strategic position again. Then, lifting his body as well as he could, he gained a firmer grip of the edge of the stirrup.

He made a faint sound in the hollow of his throat, and the mare moved. The strain of the starting almost disengaged his hold, but the strength that was in all parts of his body was not lacking in the mighty grasp of his jaw. Like the bulldog to which old Doc Adler had compared him, he kept his hold, and the mare dragged him over the grass.

She stopped. He heard the rattle of her bridle as she shook her head. Again he groaned forth a stifled order, and again she went on. She stepped forth at a brisk walk, and his body slid easily over the grass.

Every step from that lean-to was a step toward salvation. And with a vast incredulity he found himself drawn up to the verge of the brush, and then through a gap in it. He had taught her to go by gee and haw. Those words he used now, bringing them out of his throat without much difficulty in spite of the fact that his teeth were locked. So he guided her well to the left. For straight above them would be those waiting watchers of the gang of McGregor; and he would have to attempt to cut around to the side of them.

His hope was to find the other men—the group of six who were searching the trail!

So he guided her, and she dragged him steadily up until they came to the rocks.

Half a dozen times, a projecting stone caught at his shoulder and broke the grip of his teeth. A tooth snapped off short. Blood filled his mouth. But he was hardly sensible of it, or of the pain.

Faith, which had been born in him full-grown in the shed, in the presence of death, had grown to a giant in his soul, now that he had the hope of life. Again and again he resumed his grip on the stirrup leather, and again and again the mare, having lost him, came back to his voice. She began to learn her work. She began to avoid obstacles against which she might drag that precious burden which trailed behind.

A sound of steps came near him. He stopped the mare with a whisper and lay still. Horses were moving by him. He saw nothing, but he heard the grinding of the iron shoes against the rocks.

Then two voices.

"They won't find nothin'."

"If they do, we'll be gone."

"McGregor's killed Peary."

"Yeah. But Peary's the lucky one, I reckon."

And they laughed, both of them!

But the night covered the sound of the horses rapidly. Once more Barney could resume that strange progress. It brought him up, at last, onto the trail. The clothes on his back and sides had been ripped to tatters. His flesh was raw in many a place. But that hardly mattered, when he saw far away the gleam of a light. Whoever searched that trail was not a friend of McGregor. That was certain, and that was all he wished to know. So he raised his voice to a shout, to a thundering outcry that beat far away in echo on echo. "Help! Help! This way! Help!"

The light staggered and disappeared. There was a rush of hoofbeats. He shouted again, and suddenly around him was a swirl of horsemen.

"Who's there?" called the voice of Parmelee.

"Barney Dwyer!" he answered.

They gave one wild yell of satisfaction and rage, commingled. In an instant he was free, he weas lifted. Furious inquiries poured on him.

But Barney was already in the saddle on the red mare.

"Parmelee," he said, "Loftus was a liar. McGregor sent him. I suppose that Sue's letter was forged. But down there in a shack is Peary—and perhaps some of the rest of them."

And he added: "Will you follow me?"

"To hell and back!" shouted the voice of Red.

And Barney drove the mare frantically back over the ground he had just covered so painfully inch by inch!

They swept through the brush and rocks, and they came beating out on the level of the grass.

Were the men of McGregor waiting for the attack, hiding like so many Indians? No, but far away the hoofs of their horses were pounding!

From the shed burned the light of the lantern, still. That was the first goal. Out of the saddle, and into the doorway, in time to see a frightful picture of poor Len Peary lifting himself from the floor, with glazed eyes like the eyes of the dead, and a horrible red wound that slanted from the center of his forehead up into his hair. It must have been a glancing wound. There was no other explanation for the life in that half-conscious body.

But the life was there. That was the main thing. The life was in him; and yonder were the beating hoofs of the horses that carried the men of McGregor away. They must not escape! It was not mere anger that filled Barney. It was a coldness of resolution, like the coldness of steel.

"Leave one man, Parmelee,' he begged, "and the rest come on with me. I've got to find McGregor before this trail ends!"

There was not a man of them all who did not ride as well as his horse would carry him on that night. But the difference was that their horses galloped and the red mare flew. And a ragged half-moon rose in the east and looked down the narrow ravine through which the men of McGregor were fleeing.

Barney was hardly aware that his friends were dropping behind him. He only knew that he was gaining rapidly on the scurrying forms that ran ahead.

Two of them rode side by side, last of all. Would they fight? Not they! Well had Peary announced the quality of those who followed the diminished fortunes of McGregor now! Barney had snatched a revolver that was thrust into his hands by one of the men from the Parmelee ranch—Red, was it not?—and now he fired high in the air.

The two rascals nearest at hand screeched as though the bullet had driven through both their bodies. They drew up and turned, and lifted their hands high above their heads, and yelled for mercy.

But Barney drove headlong past them.

They were nothing. They were the ciphers without meaning, once McGregor was removed.

And McGregor was there.

Off to the sides scurried three more, before the charge of the red mare, and now remained only two. He could swear that they were the great McGregor and terrible old Doc Adler.

But even Adler hardly mattered. He was old, and time would soon end him, no doubt. But McGregor was young. He must be slain as a wolf is slain when there are sheep in the pasturelands.

The small ravine gave into a larger one with great broken walls that fenced, high above them, a narrow street through the sky, but still the valley held toward the east, and therefore the moon shone down into it.

And still the red mare gained, running with a deathless courage, faster and faster, as though she understood very well the meaning of this race. She did not need watching. She would pick her footing among the loose rocks that were scattered over the floor of the valley. No wild mountain goat could be surer of foot than was she.

But not so one of the nearing horses of the pair ahead. It staggered, toppled, and leaped again to its feet. On the ground, prostrate, remained the long body of Adler, with the moon glinting on his hair. He was raising himself, crawling slowly to his feet, as though stunned, when Barney drove past. Nothing could have been easier than to drive a bullet through that murderous old man, but the finger of Barney Dwyer would not close over the trigger.

A strange passion came over him. There was a roar of water from the deeps of the ravine. It entered his brain like the shouting of voices. The moon seemed to him to be hung divinely in the sky to give him light for his purpose. There was no doubt in him. It seemed to him now that from the first he had been merely a tool to be used in breaking McGregor. And now he would finish the work. He would have charged on if a hundred men were there to stand beside the bandit.

The red mare knew that the end was near. She redoubled her efforts as the fugitive's horse began to lose strength. Twice McGregor turned his head. Then he pulled up and turned his horse, and the long barrel of his rifle flashed in the moonlight as he unsheathed it.

He might as well have made a gesture with a straw, as far

as Barney was concerned. For he drove straight in, balancing his revolver for the distant shot.

The rifle bullet sang past his head, with the clap of the report behind it.

Still he closed on McGregor, with the revolver poised and ready in his hand.

A second time the rifle spoke, and again the fickle moonlight made McGregor miss.

But before the third chance for McGregor, Barney Dwyer fired.

It seemed as though horse and man had been slain outright, they dropped in such a heap. But it was only the mustang that had suffered with a bullet through the head.

As Barney came up, he saw McGregor struggle free, stagger, and then turn to fight his last. If the revolver ever came into the magic hand of McGregor, there could only be one termination to the battle, and Barney, as he swung out of the saddle, gripped the outlaw with both hands.

As a great electric current could paralyze a strong man, so McGregor was paralyzed. He struggled vainly. He flung his head from side to side. But Barney held him like a child.

At last McGregor knew, and stood still. Only his face worked, as words came up to his lips and were denied utterance. What could he say?

"Barney," he gasped at last, "for God's sake give me a last chance. I would have murdered you. But you were ready to die. And I'm no more ready than a black dog. Barney, don't kill me with those hands of yours!"

"McGregor," said Barney, "don't whine. You've lived and fought and killed. You've been what you thought a man should be. You ought to die like a man. And I've got to kill you!"

"Don't kill me, Dwyer!" shouted McGregor. "Barney, I can make you rich. I've got enough money—"

Unable to meet the terror in that face, Barney had looked away, down the smooth descent of rock on which they stood to the verge of the creek's channel, where the spray leaped like the pale lashes of a thousand whips.

Now, with a groan of disgust, he suddenly stepped back

and thrust McGregor from him, exclaiming: "You're not fit
to live, McGregor, but in my mind, you're not fit to die,
either. I can't kill a coward!"

So he had exclaimed, casting McGregor from him, and
hearing the outlaw groan with relief.

Then chance took its turn in the game. That slope of rock
to the verge of the inner ravine was wet and slippery with the
spray that had been thrown up by the stream, and the boots of
McGregor slipped on the surface as though it were oiled.

He put down a hand to stop the sliding. It was in vain.
Suddenly he realized that he was barely set free from death in
one way, to be delivered to it in another.

He cast himself facedown, spreading out his arms with
such a screech as Barney Dwyer would never forget.

But the descent was too swift, and the surface of the rock
too slippery. A jutting rock stopped the slide of McGregor for
an instant and brought him to his feet. But he reeled backward. For an instant he beat at the air with his hands and his
terrible face was silvered by the moon for Barney to see.
Then he was gone.

Barney, shaking in all his body, worked his way down to
the edge of the rock.

That was where the men from the Parmelee ranch found
him—stretched prone and looking down into the furious
uproar, the wild beating of the water and the leaping of the
foam.

They had gathered in the gang of McGregor as fishermen
gather up little fish from the sea. Only old Doc Adler had
slipped through their fingers.

But Barney Dwyer felt no exultation. He was silent all the
way into the town of Coffeeville, where the Parmelee cowpunchers brought their prisoners.

The moon turned into a pale tuft of cloud before they
reached the town. The dawn began. In the rose of it they
entered Coffeeville, but not too early to be seen and observed.

So the news ran riot through the little place. McGregor was
dead! He had escaped only to die at once, more horribly than
the death which the law would have given him.

McGregor was dead. Doc Adler, alone, would hardly be

more than a fangless snake, to be sure. And as for the harm done by McGregor's last efforts, there was only Leonard Peary to account for, and he was now lying in the hospital in Coffeeville, recovering as fast as rest and medicine could make him.

He would be marked for life, to be sure. But, as he said to Barney Dwyer: "I had it coming to me. If I hadn't been marked, it would have been wrong. I deserved a lot worse than I got."

Barney studied that thought, but finally he shook his head.

"I don't know," he said. "There's justice, somewhere, and there's a judge. I felt it out there in the lean-to. I felt that I was being judged, and McGregor and Adler were being judged. And no matter what we do or how far or how fast we run, we never can get away from *that* sort of a judgment, Len!"

He stood up.

"My father's in the next room. He wants to see you," said Peary.

Barney considered.

"I used to think," he said at last, "that I wanted nothing so much as to get back there to the ranch, and be among those cowpunchers again. But I've been changing my mind, Len. I've changed my mind about a lot of things. I don't blame people for what they used to do to me. But I don't want to see them again. You tell your father that, and I think that he'll understand.

He went down the stairs and to the back of the hotel. Through the back door he escaped into the lane, and so, by devious paths, afraid that the crowd might see him, he returned to the house of Dr. Swain.

Sue Jones was sitting up straight in her easy chair in the garden. And Robert Parmelee was sitting beside her, talking hard and fast, making eager gestures, leaning toward her.

A certain coldness came over the mind of Barney. For Parmelee talked like a man making love, and the girl listened as though she were moved to her heart, for her eyes were closed and there was a tender smile on her lips.

Slowly Barney approached.

Big Parmelee stood up and greeted him.

"I've got the whole future blocked out, Barney," he said. "You're going up there and take a part of my land. That's to be your beginning. Rustling is going to die; the rustlers are going to clear out, when they know that you're around. You'll be my foreman on a fat salary, and you'll boss your own herds, and Sue will boss you. Tell me, Barney, if that makes a happy future?"

Barney Dwyer smiled, but looked quickly at the girl. She did not even open her eyes, but held out a hand toward him.

"What do you say to it, Sue?" he asked her.

"Nothing," said the girl. "I don't care what happens, or what we do. We could sit and drift, I think, and everything would be sure to come out right in the end. These mountains were made for you, and you were made for the mountains. Any other air is too thick for a mountain man."

Max Brand is the best-known pen name of Frederick Faust, creator of Dr. Kildare, Destry, and many other fictional characters popular with readers and viewers worldwide. Faust wrote for a variety of audiences in many genres. His enormous output, totaling approximately thirty million words or the equivalent of 530 ordinary books, covered nearly every field: crime, fantasy, historical romance, espionage, Westerns, science fiction, adventure, animal stories, love, war, and fashionable society, big business and big medicine. Eighty motion pictures have been based on his work along with many radio and television programs. For good measure he also published four volumes of poetry. Perhaps no other author has reached more people in more different ways.

Born in Seattle in 1892, orphaned early, Faust grew up in the rural San Joaquin Valley of California. At Berkeley he became a student rebel and one-man literary movement, contributing prodigiously to all campus publications. Denied a degree because of unconventional conduct, he embarked on a series of adventures culminating in New York City where, after a period of near starvation, he received simultaneous recognition as a serious poet and successful popular-prose writer. Later, he traveled widely, making his home in New York, then in Florence, and finally in Los Angeles.

Once the United States entered the Second World War, Faust abandoned his lucrative writing career and his work as a screenwriter to serve as a war correspondent with the infantry in Italy, despite his fifty-one years and a bad heart. He was killed during a night attack on a hilltop village held by the German army. New books based on magazine serials or unpublished manuscripts continue to appear. Alive and dead he has averaged a new one every four months for seventy-five years. In the U.S. alone nine publishers issue his work, plus many more in foreign countries. Yet, only recently have the full dimensions of this extraordinarily versatile and prolific writer come to be recognized and his stature as a protean literary figure in the 20th Century acknowledged. His popularity continues to grow throughout the world.